You ar̲e̲... ...ding

Jack ...ter

at the

Paradise Hotel,

Hawaii

The groom will be attended by

Doubt, Trepidation…

and an unexpected baby

left on his doorstep by

the beautiful (and unmarried)

Dani Carpenter

The bride will be…present, we hope

Please join us for this joyful occasion

We are assured that the weather reports

are greatly exaggerated.

Dear Reader,

We're so glad you could join us in beautiful Hawaii for what promises to be a perfect wedding! But wait—let's hear it from the mother of the bride herself, Babs Brewster.

"If only they'd listened to me, none of this would've happened. Now Stephanie is about to miss her own wedding, and her fiancé, Jack, is imagining he's in love with that girl in the Big Bird outfit! And what I really want to know is what he is doing with a baby! And if that's not enough, I hear there's a hurricane coming and we'll probably all be washed out to sea! I ask you, what's a mother to do?"

You're about to find out as we bring you the first of THREE WEDDINGS & A HURRICANE, a hilarious new trilogy from friends Debbi Rawlins, Jo Leigh and Karen Toller Whittenburg. Be sure you don't miss out on a single minute of the fun. Watch for the next two books—*Quick, Find a Ring!* and *Please Say "I Do"*—coming to you in the next two months.

Happy reading!

Debra Matteucci
Senior Editor & Editorial Coordinator
Harlequin Books
300 East 42nd Street
New York, NY 10017

MARRY ME, BABY

DEBBI RAWLINS

Harlequin Books

TORONTO • NEW YORK • LONDON
AMSTERDAM • PARIS • SYDNEY • HAMBURG
STOCKHOLM • ATHENS • TOKYO • MILAN
MADRID • WARSAW • BUDAPEST • AUCKLAND

This is dedicated to Barbara Quattrone, a better mother-
in-law than even I could have made up. Thanks for all
your unfailing love and support.

And to my fabulous critique partners and fellow trilogy
writers—Jo Leigh and Karen Toller Whittenburg.
Thanks for making my life such a joy.

ISBN 0-373-16691-5

MARRY ME, BABY

Copyright © 1997 by Debbi Quattrone.

Chapter One

"How does it feel to be a trophy husband?"

Jack Keaton muttered a curse, and sent his best man a warning look before tipping his beer to his lips and taking a long pull.

Gritting his teeth, he set the empty bottle back on the soggy cocktail napkin and signaled the bartender for another round, not bothering to point out that he wasn't a husband yet. He wasn't going to let his friend goad him.

"You *do* know that's all you'll be to her," Rik said, before licking the salt from his fisted hand, then tossing back a shot of tequila.

Jack squinted at him. Either the light had gotten brighter in the open-air hotel bar or Jack'd had one too many beers. "As a best man you really stink."

Rik shook his head, his expression serious. "I'm your friend and partner first. And I'm telling you this marriage is a big mistake. A really big mistake."

Jack thought his friend's words were a little slurred, but his own head had gotten slightly fuzzy and he wasn't sure. "Ex-partner," he reminded him.

Rik frowned. "Is that what's eating you? My retirement?"

"Hell, no." He straightened on the bar stool and stared out toward the ocean. Dark clouds obscured the blue Hawaiian sky. "I don't blame you for getting out. I would, too, if I could. Guiding is a young man's business." He smiled back at the blond bartender who set down another bottle of beer in front of him. She was pretty, though not nearly as pretty as his fiancée, Stephanie. He should be a happy man. He wasn't. "It's a jungle out there."

They both laughed at the pun. Then Rik propped an elbow on the bar and said, "You'll never leave the Amazon. You don't know how to live in civilization anymore."

"I don't know. That hotel mattress felt pretty good the past two nights. I could get used to it."

"You're a damn liar." Rik squirted lime juice onto his wrist, sprinkled on salt, licked it off then gulped down his fourth shot of tequila.

Uneasy with the conversation, Jack rubbed the back of his neck. "What's your problem, Austin? You never drink this much. You act like you're the one getting married."

Rik snorted. "This is it. I'm cut off. No more booze." He pushed the empty shot glass, the lime wedges and saltshaker to the far side of the bar. Then he raised his bloodshot blue eyes to Jack's. "You don't drink much either. Admit this marriage is a mistake."

Jack exhaled, shoving aside the rest of his beer. "Stephanie and I both know what we're walking into. She needs a husband. It's no big deal." Jack slumped in his chair. "Besides, it's not like this is screwing up any other marriage plans. So what gives? I thought you liked her."

"She's an ice princess. You guys have zero in common."

Jack's temper flared. People often misunderstood Stephanie. He'd known her for thirty-two years. Her family had moved next door the year he'd started kindergarten. Stephanie was born soon after. Throughout the years, they had alternately fought and played together, but he'd always defended her. It seemed old habits died hard.

"We all had a damn good time when she came down to visit last year," he said. "Why the doom and gloom sermon now?"

"You're not the marrying kind. You'll break too many hearts. And living several thousand miles apart is a damn stupid way to run a marriage anyway." Rik waved an unsteady hand. "As your best friend, I'm duty-bound to tell you this is ridiculous," he said seriously, and Jack had to smile. His best man was going to have one helluva headache.

The simple act of making his lips curve made Jack cringe, and he rubbed his throbbing left temple. So was he. "Let's get out of here, huh?"

Rik glanced at his watch, then quickly grabbed the check and scribbled his name across the bottom. "Man, I didn't think you'd go through with this."

Neither had he, Jack admitted to himself, his gaze wandering toward the darkening horizon. He'd half-heartedly accepted Stephanie's proposal, never thinking it would come to this. He knew she was in a bind, that she had to find someone suitable to marry, but he'd truly thought she'd find another way out of her problem. He'd about croaked when he received an invitation to his own wedding.

The wind picked up off the beach and whipped

through the open bar. A coconut hat flew off a balding man's head and sailed toward the trio singing Hawaiian songs in the corner. An elderly lady's pink floral dress billowed and knocked a glass off a nearby table, sending a waitress scrambling for the broken glass.

"Are the forecasters still predicting that the storm will miss us?" Rik asked, eyeing the ugly black clouds gathering over the ocean.

"Last I heard."

"Maybe you'll luck out and the island will sink."

Shaking his head, Jack pushed himself off the stool. "Get over it, Austin. In forty-eight hours, I'm going to be a married man."

"You forgot happily, Jack." Rik grabbed his room key off the bar, and with a grim face, followed him to the door. "Most guys woulda said happily married man."

"Oh, yeah. Right." He breathed in a supply of his waning freedom. He'd have to remember the happy part.

No way in hell would he embarrass Stephanie.

DANI CARPENTER stumbled out of her VW bug and nearly tripped over her large webbed feet. Sighing, she steadied herself, then slammed the creaking, rusty door.

In the past week, she'd been a belly dancer, Tinkerbell and a clown. Impersonating Big Bird was no improvement. Smoothing her bright yellow polyester feathers with one hand while tucking the head under her arm with the other, she figured it could have been worse. Barney had been the customer's first choice. Luckily, she'd demolished the purple costume at a birthday party last week.

The hotel parking lot was full. A trade wind whirled

between cars and up her yellow tights. It wasn't a particularly cool breeze, pretty warm and normal for June on Maui, but it sent a shiver through her nevertheless.

She swept her windblown ponytail back with her free hand. It was the audition scheduled for the day after tomorrow that was making her edgy, she told herself, glancing up at the darkening sky. An opportunity like that didn't come often. She only hoped the weather would cooperate long enough for her to make it to Honolulu.

Tossing back her hair, she ignored the strange glances from people milling about, and marched through the lobby toward the concierge desk. There was no question about it. She was going to make it to her audition if she had to swim to Honolulu.

"Excuse me?" Dani waited for the dark-haired woman to look up from her desk calendar.

The young woman blinked in surprise, her gaze drifting from Dani's face to her feathered shoulders. "You must be delivering Mr. Keaton's singing telegram," she said, a smile forming. When Dani nodded, the smile wavered and the woman glanced from left to right. "I'm Carla. Follow me. I'll get the, uh, package you need to give him."

Dani had a bad feeling about this. If this wasn't one of Maui's premier resorts, she'd certainly think twice about following the petite and obviously nervous woman down the narrow hall.

But a job was a job, and within seconds, they arrived at an office at the back of the lobby. The concierge ducked inside, then emerged with a basket cradling a green fuzzy bundle...that gurgled.

"What was that?" Dani frowned at the sound, then

sniffed the air. It smelled like baby powder. She took a step back.

"You have to go to Mr. Keaton's room right now. If you don't, I can't be sure he'll still be there." The woman pushed the basket at Dani while glancing nervously past her down the hall.

"What am I delivering?" Her eyes narrowing, Dani shrunk farther back, fisting her hands and crossing them over her chest.

Deep male voices rumbled from somewhere behind her. Carla's eyes widened in alarm and she pushed the green fuzzy bundle at Dani. "Look, you gotta take this. If you don't I could be fired. Room five-five-five."

The voices grew louder. The bundle gurgled. Carla's large brown eyes swam in panic.

"Ohhhh." Dani muttered in disgust. When was she going to quit being such a pushover? After jerking Big Bird's head atop her own, she held out her arms.

Carla deposited the basket with enthusiasm. "Remember. Room five-five-five." She pointed down the opposite hall, then hurried toward the approaching voices.

"Sure, no problem," Dani called after her, shaking her head. The bundle gurgled...and squirmed. She lowered her incredulous gaze to the wriggling blanket. "Oh, God, please let this be a puppy."

Torn between wanting to hold it at arm's length and taking a peek at what she'd gotten herself into, Dani cradled the basket to her chest with one arm and nudged aside the green blanket.

The baby's mouth widened into a yawn as a miniature fist shot into the air. Its eyes opened and twin brown almonds stared back. Then its tiny pink lips puckered into a disgruntled pout.

Oh, heaven help her, it was going to start crying.

THE PLEASANT BUZZ was dimming. A hangover would come next. Although it had been over a decade since Jack had gotten this soused, he remembered the drill.

Actually, he wasn't really soused. It would take more than four beers to do that. But in his present frame of mind, even one had done a number on him.

A hangover would serve him right, he thought as he pulled off his shirt and doubled the pillows on his king-size bed. The same bed he'd be sharing with Stephanie in two nights.

A mild wave of queasiness moistened the skin over his temples. He did a U-turn and headed for the aspirin in his shaving kit.

A knock sounded at the door as he got halfway to the bathroom, and he cursed at the humming air conditioner. He thought Rik would be sound asleep by now.

"What do—" He threw open the door.

A blur of yellow filled the doorway. A big yellow nose…no, a beak angled up at him.

He blinked, rubbed his eyes.

It was still there. A bird. A big damn bird.

He frowned. "Rik?"

"Mr. Keaton?"

The voice was feminine, soft, practically a whisper. Jack leaned against the doorjamb, shaking his head, rubbing his bare chest. The beak angled down while several moments of silence lapsed. Then it snapped back up.

"Are you, or are you not Mr. Keaton?" The voice wasn't soft anymore. It was short, impatient. Yellow-stockinged legs shifted restlessly.

"Yeah, I'm Jack Keaton. What's going on?"

The bird cleared its throat. One lone shrill note pierced the air, then the oversize stork burst into song.

If you could call it that. Jack cringed and put a hand to his forehead. Other than being able to identify the words *congratulations* and *your turn* the tune was totally unrecognizable, the high notes missed by a jungle mile.

"I give up." He put up a hand, pleading for silence. "Take whatever you want. My wallet's on the dresser."

The bird stopped. "Actually, Mr. Keaton," it said cheerfully, "I'm not taking anything. I'm dropping something off. But there is another chorus and little dance that goes with—"

"I won't tell anyone if you don't." Shaking his head, he reached into his pocket and withdrew a handful of bills. Rik had been in the jungle too long. The least he could have done was send him a stripper or something. "Sorry I don't have any sunflower seeds."

"Cute." The bird ducked.

"Hey." Jack started to shove a tip at it before it left. God knew it could use it. Singing for its supper was not an option.

But its big, bulky feathered body blocked the doorway as it suddenly stooped to the floor, nearly sending Jack somersaulting into the corridor. He grabbed the door frame and steadied himself, his stomach protesting.

"What kind of bird are you, a cuckoo?" He pressed a hand to his gut, willing the churning to stop.

"No," the bird bounced up, a large basket in its hand. "A stork."

He frowned at the green fuzzy blanket. A stork? This was getting weirder by the minute.

"Here's the note that goes with it. I have to go now."

The basket hit him waist level. Automatically, he put his hands out.

"You got it?"

The edgy panic in the stork's voice stirred his unease. He quickly withdrew his hands. "What is it? And why are you whispering?"

"Look, mister, you have all day to figure that out. I'm paid by the hour. Take your package."

"What if I don't want to accept it?"

"That's between you and the person who signed the note."

Jack's gaze drifted to the small white envelope sitting atop the green blanket-like covering. Something moved.

"Hey." He backed up.

The stork advanced into the room. "I'm going to set it down right here."

Jack grabbed the bird's arm midway to the floor. "Flip back that covering."

"That's beyond my job description."

"So is singing. Flip it back."

"I'm going to ignore that remark." The bird snatched back its arm. "Okay, but you hold the basket."

"What do you think I am, stupid?"

"I don't know you that well, but if you want me to guess—"

"Show me what's in the damn basket, or take it with you." What the hell was he doing talking to a walking cartoon? He kicked the door shut, blocking any chance of escape. A strange gurgling sound came from the basket. "Now."

"Okay, but whatever's in there won't change anything."

The bird had breasts, he realized. Full and round, they rose and fell under the absurd yellow feathers as she cradled the basket to her waist.

He shook the sudden and irrational urge to see her face and pointed to the basket. "Let's see."

He heard her intake of breath. Her breasts rounded high, and her small yellow-gloved hand hesitated at the edge of the blanket. "Do you want to read the note first?"

He glared at her. She shrugged and gently folded back the blanket.

He blinked. Eyes closed, a towheaded baby drooled in its sleep. Jack was hallucinating. That had to be the only explanation. He glanced up at the bird. Its shiny yellow beak and bright plastic eyes were aimed at the baby.

"What is it?" he asked.

The beak raised with an exasperated sigh. "Keep your voice down."

"Is it yours?"

"No, it's not mine." She tried to push the basket at him. "I'm just the messenger."

He took a step back. And then another. "Well, it's not mine."

She paused, the beak only inches from the basket. "It looks like you."

"Give me that note." Jack snatched the envelope, his knees getting a little weak.

The card was plain and white. In feminine-looking

pink script it said *It's your turn to be a parent, Jack. Take care of Sam.*

He flipped the card over. It wasn't signed. This had to be meant for some other Jack. His brain scrambled for any possibility that the child was his. But he'd been deep in the Amazon jungle for the past three years. And although he hadn't lived the life of monk while down there...

"There's been a mistake." He tried stuffing the card back into the envelope and succeeded only in mangling the note and getting two paper cuts. He shoved the message at her.

She sidestepped him and set the basket on the bed. "Oh, no. My job is done."

"You can't leave that here."

"Yes, I can." She headed for the door.

He jumped in her way. "Take off that costume."

"Excuse me?" She dodged him on the right.

"I want to see what kind of woman would leave her child with a stranger."

"What?" She stopped and spun on him, her padded yellow belly still jiggling from the motion. It suddenly struck him how funny this would be if the situation were different—if it were happening to someone else.

"Oh, no. I'm not falling for this." She got to the door and her hand hesitated on the knob. "What did the note say?" she asked slowly.

Jack walked over and handed it to her. From the tone of her voice, her curiosity seemed both reluctant and genuine. What exactly was her role in this sick joke? He didn't know what to think. But he wasn't going to find out a thing with that foolish getup masking her expression.

"Could you take off the, uh..." He gestured at the ridiculous head gear.

"What?" She touched the beak. "Oh, yeah, it's getting hot under here." She gripped the edge of the material and bending slightly forward, pulled off the feathered helmet.

A thick rope of black hair flipped into the air before falling heavily across her cheek. She threw back her head and the disheveled ponytail settled on her shoulder. Dark spiraling tendrils framed a pair of startling green eyes that gleamed with distrust. She aimed them squarely on him.

"You really don't know that baby?" she asked, her gaze darting to the basket. She yanked off one of the gloves and with a pale slender hand, brushed away the strands of hair clinging to her face.

"Not at all. Where did you get him?"

"It's a him?" Smiling, she moved closer to the bed and peered into the basket. The baby peeked out of sleepy eyes and raised a tiny fist in the air.

"His name is Sam." He pointed to the note she still held in her hand.

Her eyes stayed glued to the baby. "But is that Sam as in 'Samuel' or Sam as in 'Samantha'?"

"Samuel, I guess."

Her gaze met his. "So, you *do* know the baby."

"No, damn it. I'm simply assuming it's Samuel."

"Why would you do that? He could be a she."

"It doesn't matter. We'll just call it Sam."

"It?" She put a hand on her hip as her gaze roamed his face. Her eyes, a crisp cool green as clear as fine-spun glass, told him as plainly as the tiny beauty mark showed at the corner of her mouth, just what she thought of him.

Well, he'd been called scum before. He scratched his stubbled jaw. He hadn't shaved in two days, and he was three weeks overdue for a haircut. No doubt he looked like hell.

Tough. He hadn't been expecting company. Stephanie wasn't due until tomorrow.

Stephanie? "Oh, hell. You gotta get this baby out of here."

"First, we have to find out if it's a boy or girl." She started to unfold the note.

"How are we going to do that?"

Her hands stilled and she looked up at him with those incredible green eyes. "You'll have to look."

He nodded, and started toward the baby. I'll have to... Stopping midstride, he turned a frown on her. "I'm not going to *look*."

She stared down at the unfolded piece of paper, before shock, then anger widened her gaze on him. "You *are* the father."

This was worse than a hangover. "I am nobody's father. Someone has made a very big mistake."

Her eyes grew brighter by the second, a faint pink seeping into her complexion. With an impatient hand, she pushed an escaped lock of glossy black hair off her face. "You are a despicable excuse for a human being."

The satiny darkness of her hair was a remarkable contrast to her eyes and fair skin. And it occurred to Jack that this wasn't the time to be noticing how pretty she was. But despicable? "Lady, you're jumping the gun here—"

"This poor baby..." Her voice had started to rise and she quickly lowered it. "This poor innocent—"

It was too late. Sam scrunched up his—or her—face

and let out a yowl. The bird lady's look of horror slid into anger as her gaze moved from Sam to Jack. "See what you've done?"

"Me?" Jack pressed fingertips to his throbbing head and briefly closed his eyes. "Well, pick it up or something."

"You do it. You'll need the practice." She cast an anxious glance at the baby, her yellow-gloved hand intertwining with the bare one.

He'd wait her out. Jack knew she wouldn't let the baby cry for much longer. He hooked his thumbs into the loops of his jeans and braced himself against the unfamiliar noise.

Her eyes followed the action of his hands, then lingered on his bare belly. He had scarcely resisted the urge to suck it in before she raised her gaze to his.

She blinked. "I'll get the baby. You put on a shirt."

He grinned. "Yes, ma'am."

She gave him a scathing look as she bent to scoop up the infant. "My name is Dani. Not that I'll be around long enough for you to use it."

"Right. You've got to return the baby."

Sam quieted as soon as Dani hugged him to her breasts. He grabbed a fistful of the yellow feathers poking off her shoulder and issued a gurgling sound.

She made a face. "I think your son is wet."

"Damn it. He's not my son. I've never seen this kid before in my life."

"How old is he?" she asked as she rooted around in the contents of the basket while balancing Sam in her other arm.

Jack threw up his hands and glanced around the room. "All right. Where are the cameras?"

She arched a confused brow and continued searching through the basket.

"Rik put you up to this, didn't he?"

She withdrew something rolled up and white, then turned to frown at him. Only her gaze drifted lower, toward his chest and the scowl disappeared as she caught her lower lip with even white teeth.

"I don't know any Rik." She turned to lay the baby on the bed. "I don't even know who ordered the telegram. My office would." Without looking up, she added. "Your shirt?"

He swept aside a stack of newspapers. Half of them fell off the bed onto the floor. No shirt. "What's the phone number?"

"Um, there's a more pressing matter here." She held up the white cloth she'd withdrawn from the basket and dangled it in the air.

He cringed. It was definitely a diaper.

"Besides, my office will be closed by now." She threw the diaper at him.

He caught it with a clammy hand. "I'll give you a hundred dollars."

"No way."

"Two hundred."

She sneered with disgust. "Here you are ready to throw your money around and I bet you haven't paid one penny of child support."

Jack shook his head. This wasn't really happening. He was in a drunken stupor, dreaming the entire thing, being punished for having doubts about his upcoming marriage.

Oh, hell. "You don't understand," he began, forcing himself to smile. He laid a conciliatory hand on her arm. "I'm getting married in two days."

Her eyes widened. Her mouth formed an O. She clamped it shut and drew her eyebrows together. "To Sam's mother?"

She was even prettier up close like this. Her skin was flawlessly smooth, her nose slightly upturned. Almost a head shorter than he, she looked up with such earnest hope that for an instant he felt like saying yes.

"No," he said, with ludicrous regret.

She snatched her arm away and managed to nab the diaper from him as well. "You really are—are—"

"Despicable?" He drove a weary hand through his shaggy hair. "Yeah, I know. Look, I'm not sure how I can convince you that I'm not this kid's father, but the most important thing is taking care of Sam. Agreed?"

She'd already started removing the wet diaper, but she gave him a grudging sidelong glance and a small nod.

"I mean, I could accuse you of abandoning him just as easily," he said, and her head shot up, her eyes like twin green daggers. He lifted a palm to silence her. "But I'm not. I believe you don't know any more than I do."

Oddly, that was true. There was no tangible reason for him to trust her except she hadn't already deserted the child or him. And then there were her eyes. They shone so clear and guileless, he didn't think she could hide anything in them.

He smiled wryly, and told himself he was a fool. "Show me how to do this diaper thing so that I can take the next turn." When she slid him another wary look, he added, "Hopefully it won't come to that."

She still didn't trust him. He could see that in the firm set of her mouth, in the slight puckering of her well-shaped brows. She handed him the bunched-up, soiled diaper. "You can start by taking this to the bathroom."

His grin faded and he swallowed. "Right."

As soon as she turned back to the baby, he held the diaper at arm's length and hurried to the sink. After he disposed of it and washed his hands, he quickly downed three aspirin. When he returned, she was still fussing with the new diaper.

"Do you know what you're doing?" he asked, narrowing his gaze at the lump of mangled cloth. He was no expert, but he'd bet twenty bucks it wouldn't stay put.

She wrinkled her nose, started to fasten one corner, then quickly changed the angle of the safety pin. "You think you can do better?"

"You don't know, do you?" He stared in disbelief at her reddening face.

Her chin lifted. "Am I supposed to just because I have breasts?"

His gaze automatically lowered to her chest. "I don't know."

She heaved a sigh of disgust and adjusted the front of her costume. Two yellow feathers fluttered to the floor. She placed the baby back in the basket and centered it on the bed. "I'm leaving now. Good luck with Sam, who *is* a he by the way."

"You can't leave me." The aspirin churned in his stomach. "Not with him."

"Watch me."

He beat her to the door, but only by a hair. The hard doorknob bit into his lower buttock muscles as he plastered himself across her escape route.

Her face took on a fierce expression and she met him nose to nose. "Get out of my way or I'll scream."

"You don't want to upset Sam."

She blinked, and he knew he had her. A whiff of violets floated up to tease him. He breathed in the pleasant scent and took hold of her arm. It felt small and fragile under the bulky costume. He was surprised to realize that he wanted to see her without all the extra yardage and feathers.

"Let's discuss this rationally," he said, massaging her arm in a soothing fashion.

"I'm counting to three," she said. "One…"

"You don't want to do that. I'm about to be married. It'll cause a scandal."

"Two…"

Damn. Her expressive green eyes stared unflinchingly, clearly telling him she meant business, and his confidence slipped. "Dani?"

She opened her mouth, her tongue peeking between her teeth as she started to form the word three. So Jack did the only thing he could.

He kissed her.

Chapter Two

As soon as Dani's lids drifted closed, she forced them open. The kiss couldn't count if she didn't close her eyes, she figured. She allowed the soft nibbling for several more seconds before she placed both hands on his chest and shoved.

He was already backed up to the door, so she didn't make much progress, except to feel his heart slamming against her palm, his heat scorching her like the summer sun. He worked outdoors, she could tell. His skin was brown, his muscles so well toned they made her palms itch.

She yanked her hands away and stumbled backward. "You are really asking for trouble, mister." She dragged the back of her hand across her mouth. Her lips tingled. Heck, she tingled all the way to her toes. "You just gave me every reason to scream my head off."

"Think of Sam," he said softly, his dark eyes never leaving hers. "You don't want to upset him. Besides, it was nothing. I only wanted to stop you. I'm not going to hurt you." He put up both hands but he stayed put.

Nothing? It was nothing? Dani had obviously been out of the dating loop too long. That kiss had nearly curled her toes. And she'd wager her long-awaited audition that he'd just been getting warmed up.

She seized a time-out by glancing at the baby. "Okay, but try something like that again and I'll not only scream but I'll lay you out flat. I know karate."

He grinned. "I'm as good as gold from now on."

She gave him a dismissive lift of her chin. She really did know karate. Although she *had* missed a couple of classes. And he had to be over six feet and outweigh her by at least ninety pounds.

"I'll give you another ten minutes." She tapped her watch, only it was under layers of polyester and feathers so the gesture lost a little effectiveness. "Then I'm out of here."

Something slapped hard against the sliding door. They both jumped and looked around in time to see a large coconut frond take another swing at the glass. Leaves and flowers already lay strewn over the tiled balcony floor. The wind suddenly howled as if admitting culpability.

"Have you heard a weather report in the last half hour?" Jack stared out at the swishing leaves and the threatening clouds, his eyebrows drawn together in concern.

She could have watched him all afternoon. He was remarkably good-looking, although she supposed some women wouldn't think so. His nose had obviously been broken a time or two, and his jaw was a little too square. But his dark brown hair and even darker eyes tickled a fancy in her that she hadn't been aware she had.

"Have you?" he repeated, directing those seductive eyes at her. "My fiancée is flying in tomorrow evening.

I'm worried she'll have trouble getting out of Honolulu.''

His words pricked her like icy rain. He was getting married. He was off-limits. "You're right," she said, inching around to the door. "We could be in for a nasty storm. I'm going to have to shove off. I've got to *get* to Honolulu. I've got an audition.''

"A what?''

He seemed so surprised she probably could have rushed the door and made it out. But his surprise riled her, too. It was laced with amusement and reminded her of all the lectures she'd had from her mother, from her so-called friends at the university.

"An audition," she restated, "as in singing and dancing.''

"Singing, huh?'' Frowning, he massaged the muscle over his left nipple. His chest was so tanned that the difference in skin colors was negligible, except his nipple beaded and drew her attention like flowers seduce bees.

She almost reminded him to put on a shirt. But she didn't want him to know that his half-naked condition bothered her. Besides, it didn't matter. She was leaving.

She casually took a couple of steps past him and curved a palm around the doorknob. She stopped. "What do you mean, *singing, huh?*''

"Oh, nothing. I, uh…'' He shook his head, his eyebrows raised innocently. "Nothing.'' Then his gaze darted to her hand gripping the knob and he gestured toward the bed. "Shall we discuss Sam?''

"I'd really love to help but—''

"You open that door and *I'll* scream.''

She laughed.

"I'm serious." He pried her hand off the knob, took hold of her arm and walked her away from the door. "I'm a desperate man. Besides, you promised me ten minutes."

"Put on your shirt." She should leave. Trouble was tapping her on the shoulder. She felt it all the way down to her curled toes.

He gave her an odd look. "Sure. I know it's around here somewhere." He got her a safe distance away from the door and closer to Sam, then looked under a pile of newspapers, a pair of well-washed jeans, some sporting magazines, and a family-size half-empty potato chip bag.

She folded her arms across her chest, determined that he wouldn't distract her this time. "I bet you have a whole closet full of them."

"What?" He dropped to the floor and looked under the bed. "Here we go." He hopped up and shook out a light blue T-shirt, then hesitated.

He was going to pull one of her brothers' stunts. She just knew it. Rolling her eyes, she waited. But he skipped the sniff test and slipped the shirt on over his head.

"I had just taken it off before you got here. I knew it had to be here somewhere." He frowned at her Big Bird costume. "Have you got anything on under that?"

"I beg your pardon?"

"You said that getup was hot. If you don't, and you want to take it off, I could lend you something."

The thought of wearing his clothes seemed so intimate that heat crept up her neck and into her face. Her crossed arms slackened. "That won't be necessary. I won't be here that long." It wasn't fair that she could be so disconcerted and he could look so relaxed. "Besides, I'd think your fiancée would have a problem with that.''

She didn't get the reaction she'd expected. He didn't get nervous or look the least bit sheepish. His forehead creased as he seemed to consider the ramifications of Dani's suggestion.

He nodded slowly. "Yeah, she might. See, the trouble is, I don't know everyone who might already be here for the wedding. They may recognize me, but I wouldn't know them.''

Confused, she wrinkled her nose.

"Her friends and business associates are attending. A lot of them could have already checked into the hotel, but I wouldn't know them from Adam. I only know her parents and sister. But I haven't seen the Brewsters in over fifteen years.''

She didn't understand a thing he was saying except that now she knew he'd grown edgy. He dragged a palm down his thigh and exhaled loudly.

"Why don't you know any of these people?'' she asked in spite of the fact that this was none of her business, and that she should have left over thirty minutes ago.

"I live in Brazil, on the Amazon. Stephanie lives in Honolulu. I haven't been stateside for five years and that was only for a brief visit.''

"The Amazon? As in jungle?'' Dani asked, both surprised and excited. When Sam started to fuss, she automatically moved to the bed and picked him up, her attention still fastened on Jack. "What do you do there?''

"I take people for two- and three-week hiking expeditions. I'm a helicopter pilot so I do aerial tours, too.''

"Wow." She placed a pacifier she'd found in the basket in Sam's mouth and rocked him back and forth. With a wistful sigh, she added, "That's incredible."

He shrugged. "Like anything, it gets old." He watched Sam suck greedily on the pacifier. "Did someone drop him off at your office?"

"No. I picked him up from the hotel's concierge."

"You're kidding. Why didn't you say something?" He rushed to the phone, studied the directory plate, then punched in two numbers. "We should be able to wrap this matter up in no time."

Dani gave him the name of the woman, then occupied herself with inventorying Sam's basket—diapers, a pacifier, a bottle and an assortment of other things she didn't recognize—while Jack waited silently on hold, drumming his fingers and staring out at the first onslaught of rain.

He was right, of course, she should have told him immediately that she'd picked up the baby here in the hotel. But from the moment that he'd opened the door to his room, he'd kept her off balance.

She didn't know why exactly. Although she found him physically attractive, he wasn't someone who would stop a woman dead in her tracks. Her last boyfriend was probably better looking than Jack. But for some elusive reason, she was drawn to him. Her mother would credit the alignment of moons and stars or some such thing.

With some relief, Dani thought she understood the attraction a little better now that she knew his career. It was his aura of excitement and adventure that called to her. The kind of excitement she wanted so badly she could almost taste it.

"Carla's off property."

The thud of the phone being recradled and Jack's gloomy tone brought Dani back to reality. "What does that mean?" she asked.

"Whoever answered said she'd be away from the hotel for a couple of hours. I asked if they knew anything about a baby but I could tell they thought I was nuts." Releasing a sound of disgust, he walked to the glass doors. "Besides, I got the feeling they were too preoccupied with the weather. I heard talk of the storm in the background. It didn't sound encouraging."

"Here." She hurried toward him and placed Sam in his arms. "As soon as the concierge gets back, your problem will be solved. In the meantime, I've got a storm to outrun."

"Hey, I think he needs changing again." He held the baby out with stiff arms.

"There are still a couple of fresh diapers in the basket."

"I was only kidding about the storm. I heard it was clearing—"

Sam started crying, drowning out Jack's voice.

She'd gotten within two yards of the door, but made the mistake of glancing over her shoulder. Both the males in her immediate life looked fit to be tied. Sam was beet red from screaming, and Jack was as pale as the stark white walls.

"I'm begging you, Dani," he shouted over Sam's wailing. "Don't leave me like this."

Then he brought the baby to his chest and wrapped both muscled arms around him and Sam stopped howling. He raised his tearstained face to Jack and gurgled, his tiny lips starting to curve.

Jack stared at the child for a moment, then looked up at her with the most incredulous expression, his hair falling across his forehead, his brown eyes gleaming with wonder. "I think the kid likes me."

Every bone in her body turned to tapioca as she watched Jack return his attention to Sam. He smiled at the baby, who happily cooed back, his large dark eyes shining only for Jack. She steadied herself by grasping a green upholstered rattan chair. They were the perfect picture of harmony.

And she was no longer needed.

Her fingers tightened around the polished bamboo.

The unexpected and irrational feeling of being left out was like a cloud far darker than the one dumping torrents of rain down on the resort. Where had it come from? She didn't *want* to be needed. She wanted freedom. She wanted adventure.

Her gaze rested on the Big Bird headgear she'd almost forgotten in her haste. She released her death grip on the chair, and picked up the helmet.

This was her big chance to get out of here. She allowed herself one last glance at them, then edged toward freedom.

As she slipped through the door, she wasn't sure they even heard her leave.

THE WIND HAD turned downright nasty by the time Dani made it halfway across the parking lot. Speeding gusts played havoc with the rain, driving it down in slanting sheets that stung her face and neck. Her costume soaked up the water like a sponge, until it felt like she was carrying a dozen boxes of Godiva chocolates on her thighs.

Visibility was almost nil no matter how hard she squinted. And keeping her hair from whipping across her eyes was a full-time job. This was no ordinary tropical storm, no matter what the weatherman said.

She didn't mind the challenge though. It kept her from thinking too much about Jack, the baby and...the *kiss*. How had she got into this mess? No, *that* mess. The whole scenario was past tense, she reminded herself. She'd done what she'd been paid to do, regardless of how irresponsible the task had been.

She cringed as the disturbing fact she'd been trying to keep at bay clawed at her conscience. An innocent baby was being used as a pawn in some horrible practical joke. And if that weren't the case, the alternative answer held no greater appeal. It meant that Jack really was the father, and Sam's mother saw no other way to persuade Jack to accept his responsibility.

Dani didn't want to believe that. Her instincts screamed against the possibility. But she didn't know the man at all, other than he kissed like a dream, made her knees weak, and had nearly caused Big Bird's yellow polyester to molt.

But one fact did remain certain, she reminded herself. He was an engaged man. He had no business kissing her at all. She sighed. Obviously her instincts were as reliable as the weather forecast had been.

She glanced up at the black sky as she quickened her pace. The wind slapped her face and swayed her slightly off course. Righting herself, she decided that she'd have to take an earlier flight to Honolulu. She had only one shot at this audition and she wasn't taking any chances.

The parking lot was full, hordes of rental cars and mopeds were jammed in every available spot, legal or otherwise, and it took her a little extra time to locate her car, wedged between a late model burgundy van and a pink Jeep.

After opening the driver's door as far as possible and gauging the tight squeeze it would be to slip behind the wheel, Dani reached into her small hidden pocket for her keys. The wet costume hung heavy and limp around her body and her first attempt at fishing for the two keys held together by a safety pin proved unsuccessful. She swept her fingers around the inside seam and was relieved to feel cold metal at her fingertips.

Digging deep, she grasped the object and pulled it out of her pocket. She opened her hand and stared at her house key. Not even the safety pin was still attached.

Dread coiled in her stomach. She patted frantically at her pocket before finally pulling it inside out. Yellow lint matted with rain clumped in her hand.

Her gaze flew to the ground. A gray murky puddle seeped through her webbed feet. Behind her, more puddles merged to form a small lake. She sagged against the car and let the rain pelt her heated cheeks. Where the heck was her key?

"I KNOW THERE'S an emergency." Hollering through the telephone receiver to be heard above Sam's crying, Jack waved his hand furiously through the air. "It's in this room."

He paused for a moment to let the operator respond, but at her patronizing tone he cut her off. "Ma'am, I understand that, but the storm will still be here after you help me solve *this* problem."

"Please hold," the hotel operator said crisply. "I'll see if Carla has returned to her office."

The woman was upset with him, Jack knew, but he

wasn't in any condition to be patient. Sam had been crying for the past ten minutes and neither his bottle nor a diaper change had made him happy.

On top of that, Dani had left him. Them. Jack was trying not to take her abrupt departure personally. Even though it probably was very personal. Kissing her had been a foolish thing to do. He was engaged for God's sake. His fiancée was literally on her way to say I do. So why was he still thinking about Dani's kiss?

Sam's howling impossibly rose an octave. While still cradling the phone between his jaw and his shoulder, Jack reached for him. He'd purposely placed some distance between them so that he could hear the operator, but he'd had luck quieting Sam once before by cuddling him.

When it appeared he couldn't keep contact with the phone and reach the baby, he dropped the receiver on its side and hurried to scoop up Sam. That's when he heard the soft knock at the door.

"Hallelujah." It had to be the concierge.

Sam was unimpressed. He yelled louder.

Jack opened the door ready to present her with the baby.

"What are you doing to him?" Dani asked, frowning. "I could hear him all the way to the elevators."

Wet black hair was plastered to her head. She still wore the bird outfit, feathers poking out every which way. As she crossed the threshold, her webbed feet squeaked. She couldn't look better in a thong bikini.

His thoughts tripped over the sudden visual. Where had *that* come from? He shook his head to clear the image. "Where the hell have you been?"

"Don't get me started." She waltzed past him and picked Sam's bottle up off the rattan dresser.

"I already tried that."

Ignoring Jack, she nudged the nipple at the baby's angry mouth. Immediately, his tiny lips clamped down and he started sucking greedily. "Really, Jack, that was basic parenting 101."

"I tried that," he repeated, laying Sam down on the bed to drink his bottle.

"Please tell me you've found a key attached to a safety pin," Dani said, her gaze roaming the carpet.

"A key? I've been slightly busy." He made no attempt to hide his sarcasm, his curious gaze following hers until he noticed the receiver lying at the side of the phone. "Damn."

He dove for it, hoping the operator hadn't come back on the line yet and given up when he wasn't there. It had taken him over five minutes to get her in the first place.

"Who is that?" Dani rushed to his side.

He waved for her to be quiet. "The hotel operator, I hope. Hello? Hello?"

"Ask her if they've found a key."

"Ma'am, are you there?"

"If she doesn't know, ask her to transfer you to Lost and Found."

Jack glared at Dani. "Would you be quiet?" He turned back to the receiver. "No, ma'am, not you. Did you—"

"It's a single key attached to a safety pin." Dancing up on her silly webbed toes, she moved closer.

He started to pull away. "Damn it. This is important. Would you stop—"

She pushed her face to within a breath of his as if she could see through the phone line. Her lashes were thick and black and clumped with moisture. A drop had settled on her cheekbone and Jack had the crazy urge to lick it off.

He cleared his throat and held out the phone. "Here." As soon as she took it he backed away, out of touching distance, to the opposite end of the room. Passing a weary hand over his face, he stopped to rub his chin. He needed a shave. He needed to get out of this mess.

"No, this is Dani Carpenter, but he's still here," she said into the phone, her gaze sweeping around to meet his. "I'll tell him. Wait, no, don't. I need Lost and Found." Her words came out in a rush, her hand gripping the receiver until her knuckles turned white.

"I've lost a key," she said more calmly, when she'd obviously reclaimed the operator's attention. "My car key. Within the last hour." Her eyebrows raised in inquiry to him at the same time.

Jack shrugged and leaned against the sliding glass door. Outside, the wind howled at his back. Waves pounded the beach. The lights flickered. Dani's wary eyes clouded as she looked past him out the window.

So that's why she'd come back. Not for Sam. Not for him. Which shouldn't have bothered Jack, but it did, he admitted as he continued to watch her.

Her eyes really were a spectacular shade of green, mossy and bright at the same time, much like the jungle right after a cleansing rainfall. She moistened her bottom lip and the swift heat of memory had him aching to kiss her again.

Pushing away from the glass, he swallowed hard. As much as he needed her help with Sam, he needed to get rid of her more. He was about to be married to a woman who deserved his loyalty. And Dani was getting under his skin.

He dropped to his knees, ignoring her perplexed look and started to comb the tan carpeting. He'd find her damn key. Then she could leave and he'd never see Dani Carpenter again. He'd go through with this marriage, then get back to the Amazon and life would be normal. He just had to find the key.

She gasped. He looked up, hoping she'd found it.

Her face quickly drained of color. The phone dangled from her hand.

"The road to the hotel," she began, then stopped to take a deep shaky breath. "It just washed out."

Chapter Three

"What does that mean?" Jack asked as he lunged for the phone. Snagging the receiver, he put it to his mouth. "What does that mean?" he repeated to the operator but the line was already dead.

"This can't be happening." Dani sank onto the bed, and held the baby close to her.

Jack slammed the phone down in disgust. Sam started crying again.

"You don't have to take it out on us." She patted the baby's back. He hiccuped and struggled for a breath, drew it in noisily, then burped.

Jack grimaced at having upset Sam. He threw up his hands and in a calmer voice asked, "Do you mind telling me *what* I'm taking out on you?"

"The fact that we're stranded."

"Are you sure?"

"There's only one road to this hotel."

He rubbed the throbbing at his temple. "But it keeps going after the hotel. It has to lead somewhere."

She raised irate eyes over Sam's blond head. "Yeah, to a cliff."

"So that means—" He frowned. "What are you looking at me like that for? The weather is my fault?"

"I would have been long gone if it weren't for you."

"Oh, no, don't go pinning this on me. You should never have accepted that baby."

"His name is Sam." Dani's irritation dissolved into a slow curve of her lips as she tweaked the infant's chin. He gurgled and kicked his feet. But her smile faded as soon as she turned back to Jack. "I didn't have a choice."

"Of course you did. When the concierge tried to give him to you, you should have said no."

"It wasn't that simple."

"Now, it isn't simple."

She glared at him. "It is for me. He's your problem." She stood and gently pressed Sam to his chest.

Jack's arms automatically opened for the baby, who kicked one tiny foot in Jack's gut, then cooed his satisfaction.

"Look, we can't really be stranded. Let's call a truce and I'll help you think of a way out of here." He rocked Sam back and forth while following her to the door.

"I guess I don't need my keys for now, but if you find them, leave them at the front desk, will you?" she said distractedly, her gaze combing the carpet one last time.

"We can work this out." Wedging himself between her and the door, he smiled. He hoped flashing his pearly whites still held the same charm it had when he'd done those toothpaste commercials all those years ago. "I'm sure we can come to some kind of agreement."

"Get out of my way." Apparently Dani didn't think so.

He sighed. "Look—"

Someone knocked at the other side of the door. Jack started to answer it, but hesitated when he saw the eager look of impending freedom in Dani's eyes.

"It might be the concierge." She danced around him, trying to reach the knob.

"Good point." Balancing Sam, he managed to open the door and still block her escape.

"What took you so—" His hand still poised to knock, Rik's anxious expression slid into surprise. He looked slowly from Dani to Sam, back to Dani, taking in her beleaguered costume, and finally returned his gaze to Jack. "And I thought seeing double was bad."

He stepped into the room and grinned at Sam. The baby cooed and kicked. "He's a cute kid." Rik sent Dani a brief frown. "Yours?"

She promptly shook her head.

Jack peered closer at the baby. "How did you know it was a he?"

"The blue T-shirt. Who is he?"

Ah, the blue T-shirt. Dani and Jack exchanged glances. When Jack returned his attention to his friend, Rik was tickling Sam's chin, who gurgled in sheer bliss.

And genius struck Jack like a sudden thunderstorm.

He cleared his throat, then slid another look at Dani, silently willing her to play along. She cocked her head quizzically, obviously confused, but Jack decided to run with the pass anyway. "I thought you could tell us who he is."

"Me?" Rik gave the infant an extra tickle then raised narrowed eyes. "Why?"

"Because he was delivered to you."

"What?" His expression tightened, then relaxed, one brow lifting in amusement. He ran a gaze over

Dani's wet feathers and her soggy yellow tights. "By you?" he asked her.

But Dani was too busy gaping at Jack. She started to open her mouth, but he gave her a threatening look and cut her off. "Yeah. Only she came to the wrong room. Right?"

Hiking Sam up higher on his chest, he pointedly stepped closer to the door, directly blocking her path. His eyes bored into her green ones, his message loud and clear. *Play ball or you don't get out.*

She lifted her chin, and without breaking eye contact with Jack, spoke very slowly, as if carefully choosing her words. "Yes, I did deliver Sam."

Rik looked back and forth between them, and obviously missing the undercurrent, chuckled. "Come on, Jack, whose baby is it?"

He tore his gaze from Dani, still not comfortable that she wouldn't blow his plan, and sent Rik his most innocent expression. "You really don't know?"

Then he quickly passed Sam to his friend before he could protest. Rik helplessly cradled the infant to his chest. And Jack took a moment to study Dani. As hypocritical as it was, he was glad that she had hedged on backing up his story. It was obvious she was uncomfortable lying and that pleased him for some absurd reason.

When it was clear by her murderous expression that he'd stared too long, he said, "By the way, this is Dani, uh…"

"Carpenter," she said automatically. "And I was just leaving."

"Wait a minute. I'll walk you out." Jack pocketed his key.

"Hey, you can't leave me here with this kid."

"Of course not." Jack smiled. "Go ahead and take him to your room."

"Jack." Rik's voice was a pitch above a warning and he did a quick two-step toward the door, holding Sam out. "I'm sure you have a great explanation, and I'd love to hear it. But not now."

Sam scrunched up his face and let out a wail. Both men grimaced, then looked at Dani.

"What?" She spread her hands in supplication.

Rik seized the opportunity to place Sam in her arms. Dani reflexively embraced the baby.

"Look, guys, this is not part of my job—" When Sam took exception to her protest by raising his yowl a decibel, she moved him to her shoulder and gently rocked him up and down. He quieted in seconds.

"I'll see you later," Rik said, and hesitated only long enough for Jack to see fear override curiosity in his friend's eyes. He was out the door before you could say baby-sit.

"He got away." Disgusted, Jack turned to Dani. "Thanks for dropping the ball."

"First, you want me to play nursemaid, then you want me to lie for you? Mister, you are very nervy. Responsibility starts with an *R*. Look it up if you have to. Now, take this child."

"You don't know me well enough to say that. I'm a very responsible person," he said, offended by the accusation. Then he added hopefully, "But you could...get to know me. We have plenty of time."

"I'm going to lay Sam right here on the bed." She placed the baby in the center of the mattress and re-arranged the pillows to insulate him.

Guarding his post at the door, Jack noticed the trail

of soggy feathers littering the carpet. "You never did tell me what you're wearing under that."

She gave the pillows a final pat and straightened, pinning him with disbelieving green eyes. "Excuse me?"

He pointed to the carpet. "You're molting. Maybe you should get out of that getup."

Her shoulders sagged when she saw the clumps of yellow polyester. "First the Barney outfit and now Big Bird. This gig is going to end up costing me."

"I'll pay for the costume."

She smiled. "Thanks, but it's not your fault."

He knew that, but the offer was worth it to see her smile, he realized. She had a great smile, her teeth were white and straight, except for the front two which slightly overlapped.

Her lips were perfect, too. Naturally rose-colored, wide and bow-shaped. He bet she made a notable living on tips alone.

"What?" she asked, her mouth stretching further, and he realized he was smiling back.

"Want some help getting out of that?" he asked.

Her grin disappeared. "No."

Smooth, Jack. He rubbed the back of his neck. "I mean, you can use the bathroom if you want to change."

"One small problem. I only have a swimsuit on underneath."

"Ah…" Jack blinked, digesting that information. So what was the problem? A vivid image of her in an itsy-bitsy teeny-weeny polka-dot bikini flashed in his mind.

She crossed her arms over her chest and it was obvious that Jack wasn't going to get the opportunity to see for himself. He briefly wondered if it would be inappropriate to at least ask if it *was* a bikini. And what color.

"Sometimes it gets really hot under all this stuff," she said, her tone slightly defensive. "So we all just wear as little as possible."

He needed air. He glanced toward the sliding door. Coconut fronds continued to whack the glass, the wind howling through the seams. So much for opening the door.

He sucked in a breath. "The offer still stands. I could lend you something. A T-shirt maybe." He exhaled at her skeptical expression and reluctantly added, "And shorts."

"I don't know…"

"Sweatpants?" he offered with even greater reluctance, and finished lamely with, "They have a drawstring."

"That's very nice of you but I really should be going."

"You said yourself that we're stranded."

"I have to at least try to leave. Maybe someone will have a four-wheel drive and would be willing to brave it."

"You still need dry clothes." It suddenly occurred to him that he'd never see her again. That idea stank.

She shifted and the rubber webbed feet squeaked with moisture. "How would I get the clothes back to you? Oh, I guess I could mail them."

"Or I could pick them up."

"I won't be here. I'm leaving for Honolulu."

The wind blasted the building, rattling the windowpanes. He gazed out toward the crashing waves and wondered if this was an omen. The sky was inky. The song "Black Wedding" came to mind. "Not today you're not."

"I *have* to leave tonight or I'll miss the audition." She followed his gaze with a mixture of despair and helplessness.

"Maybe they'll cancel."

She brightened at the idea. "I should call."

He was glad he'd thought of it. Even as hesitant as her smile was, it lit up his own disposition. "Use my phone."

"Thanks." Her lips curved higher and she started to move forward. But she stopped suddenly and her hand shot up to cover her mouth. She spun toward him. "I have been so selfish." He frowned, and she said, "Your wedding. It could be postponed. You must be devastated."

"Yeah." He grinned. Then rearranged his face into a scowl. "Yeah, I am."

She frowned, too, obviously confused over his unguarded reaction. "I'm sure you want to use the phone, too. So you go first."

"Why?"

"Don't you want to call your fiancée?"

"Oh, sure." The part about the wedding being postponed didn't bother him a bit but he *was* concerned about Stephanie. Although there wasn't a doubt in his mind that she was safe and dry at her home in Honolulu. She wasn't an impulsive or illogical person. Every event in life was well orchestrated for her, including their upcoming marriage. "But you go first. I want you to have some peace of mind. I'll find something for you to wear."

Her frown deepened, and she looked at him as if he were the scum of the earth. "Okay."

While she grabbed the phone and started to dial, Jack checked on Sam. He'd fallen asleep, his fist at his mouth. It was a little scary, Jack thought as he paused to watch him sleep, being responsible for someone so small and helpless. After brushing the back of his finger reassuringly down Sam's soft cheek, he tackled the contents of his suitcase.

It was still sitting on the luggage rack near the bed. He hadn't bothered to transfer his clothes to the drawers. Listening to the storm raging outside, he figured his stay just might be extended. So as he dug around for something that would likely fit Dani, he piled his shirts and shorts on the bed away from the baby.

Although it didn't sound as though she was saying much, Jack tried not to listen to her conversation as he held out a yellow T-shirt. Nah, he was a little sick of that color at the moment. He threw it on one of the piles and picked up his old navy blue jersey. But he quickly discarded it. Too long. Then he made the mistake of glancing over his shoulder at her, and saw her gesture frantically to keep it out.

Damn. She was right. He was scum, but he didn't want to lend her a shirt that large. It was likely to cover everything.

He sighed, and carefully laid out the football jersey and added a pair of gray shorts. He was worse than scum. He was about to be married to Stephanie and all he could think about was what Dani looked like under all those feathers.

"When should I try again?" Dani's voice rose slightly, and he could tell she was anxious.

Jack moved the piles of clothes to the drawers and tried to ignore the funny feeling he had in his gut. He had no business being concerned for her, worrying about her feelings. Not beyond feeling the compassion any stranger would have for another. But he did.

As soon as she hung up the phone he looked her way. The news wasn't good. He could tell by the purse of her lips, by the tiny lines etched between her dark brows.

"They didn't cancel," he ventured.

"I couldn't get through."

"To Honolulu?"

"To an outside line. Only emergency calls are being patched through."

Jack's gaze strayed once more toward the stormy sky. This was getting serious. "Maybe we'd better turn on the news."

She nodded, then reached for the clothes he'd set out. "May I?"

"Sure. Take anything you want." He grasped the jersey the same time she did and their hands met. Hers was frigid. She snatched it back as if he had some kind of disease.

"I have a sweatshirt," he offered.

She shook her head. "My hands are always cold. My feet, too." She blushed, and he could tell that it was uncharacteristic of her to do so just by the way she reacted.

A hand flew to her face and she pressed it against her flushed cheeks. Her eyes darkened warily. "I don't like storms," she said, "That's why I'm babbling."

"It's turning into a nasty one, all right," he said gently, and placed his hands on her shoulders.

She jumped at his touch but she settled down as soon as she realized he only meant to guide her toward the bathroom.

"You go take a warm bath and I'll listen for the news on the radio."

She made it to the door, stopped and turned. "This is very weird, isn't it? I mean, I don't even know you. And here I—"

"I promise I'm safe," he interjected. "I'm not a pervert or some maniac. I always carry a driver's license and a bankcard. Just an average guy," he reassured her, and she started to give him one of her dazzling smiles. "I'm so safe and boring," he concluded, grinning, "I'm practically married."

She blinked, her smile flickering. "Right," she said, and promptly disappeared into the bathroom.

DANI TOWEL-DRIED HERSELF until her skin prickled. After stepping back into her bikini bottoms, she picked up Jack's jersey and eyed it critically.

What the heck was she doing in some strange man's room, about to put on his clothes?

The shirt was soft and a little faded from many washings and smelled faintly of Jack. She brought it up to her face, inhaling the musky scent. She breathed deeply, briefly closing her eyes. When she opened them, and caught her reckless reflection in the mirror, she pushed the shirt guiltily away.

He was getting married, she reminded herself, as she covered her bikini bra with the jersey. Not that she was the least bit interested in him. There was a whole world waiting for her out there. The last thing she needed was to get tied down now, after she'd given up so much to be free.

Why was she even thinking this stuff? He was a stranger. A kind stranger who had offered her some hospitality. She'd finally admitted to herself that, for the time being, she really was stranded, and whether it was because he wanted help with Sam or not, Jack was currently her best bet to stay dry and warm.

It was the wind, she decided. It was wild and frenzied, tracking in all sorts of weird energy and making her think crazy thoughts.

She groaned, pulled the shirt over her head and jerked through the neck opening. God, she hated sounding like her mother. Next thing she knew she'd be calling the psychic hotline.

Once she got the shorts over her hips, she realized they were too large and that the elastic waist was getting loose. But luckily the shirt was long and hid the fact that the shorts rode as low on her hips as her bikini bottoms. She adjusted her ensemble the best she could, and used the hair dryer attached to the wall to get a good deal of the moisture out of her hair. Her bangs and ends were still a little damp and flat when she flicked off the dryer and replaced it. But she ignored it to prove to herself that she wasn't primping for Jack.

Although the makeup she wore was minimal, she still had to rub out a couple of black smudges around the corners of her eyes. Once she was satisfied that she was vaguely presentable, she quietly opened the door to the bedroom.

She didn't see him right away, the room was so dark, and her attention was immediately drawn to the wind and rain battering the balcony.

It was even darker outside, the pummeled leaves drenched to a deep green and slashing at the glass as if pleading entry. The sound was awful, too, as the storm rallied not only the sky but the swelling waves that incessantly pounded the shore.

Dani shivered. She was lucky to be inside, to have

a safe place to wait out the worst of it, to have time to plan her next course of action. As much as she needed to get to Honolulu, she had no desire to be outside fighting the elements at the moment.

Running a hand up her arm, she dragged her gaze from the glass door and assessed the room. Her eyes were still adjusting to the semidarkness, aided by the soft glow of the television screen.

On the bed, Jack lay sprawled out, on his back, eyes closed, his head propped up by pillows, something clamped tightly in one hand.

Dani squinted into the murky light, then grinned when she realized it was the remote control. Something else sat high on his chest, in the shadows, and she pushed back the bathroom door for more light.

Freshly diapered, Sam lay on his stomach snuggled up below Jack's chin, his raised bottom cradled protectively by Jack's other hand.

She swallowed hard, and a strange sensation fluttered in her chest.

Storm or no storm, she had to get the hell out of here.

Chapter Four

"Dani?" Jack yawned around her name. "I must have dozed off." He released the remote control and rubbed one eye. "Where are you going?"

His voice was husky as if he'd done more than just doze. She smiled in spite of herself and relaxed her grip on the doorknob.

"To the front desk," she whispered. "I want to find out how the road is."

"You weren't running out on us, were you?" He gently rolled Sam over onto his back on the bed beside him. When Jack sat up, the bathroom light spilled onto his face and revealed a suspicious gleam in his eye.

She hoped he couldn't see the guilty flush that stole across her cheeks. Then she decided to come clean. "I thought about it."

He left the bed and tugged down the shirt that had bunched above his waist. But not before she caught a glimpse of tanned skin, a sprinkling of dark hair, his navel. It was an outie.

"And you've changed your mind?" he asked softly, advancing on her.

Her grip tightened on the knob. "Not necessarily."

"What can I do to convince you to stay?" He

stopped a mere foot away. This time the bathroom light revealed only half his face, but it was enough for her to see him give her the once-over. "My clothes," he said, shaking his head. "They look so…different."

Dani dragged her gaze from his face to look down at herself. The shorts were probably considerably longer on her, especially since they wouldn't cling to her waist. "Different?" she repeated cautiously.

She briefly met his intense eyes and decided it was safer to look elsewhere. Except that when she looked down again, she noticed that the jersey was clinging slightly to her damp bikini top. The soft fabric molded the tops of her breasts and creased at her cleavage. With a deep, involuntary breath, she tugged the shirt loose.

"Well, yeah…" He rubbed the side of his jaw. "Look, anything I say is gonna sound really sexist, so I'd better just shut up."

"Oh." Brilliant comeback. She shuffled her bare feet.

"You want some socks?" he asked.

Before she could answer, he grabbed her free hand, and surprised, she let go of the doorknob with her other. Once he led her near the dresser, he released her, his fingers trailing slowly away, across her palm, down her fingers, and leaving an army of goose bumps marching up her arm.

He smiled. "Obviously I don't have shoes that would fit you, but these are nice and thick and should keep your feet warm. Besides, you won't need shoes if you stay in the room."

She accepted the pair of white socks he handed her and realized what he'd done. He'd distracted her from leaving. As disgusted as she was with him, she was more annoyed with herself. Without a word, she pulled on the socks.

"Better?" he asked, still smiling.

Dani didn't feel quite as chipper as Jack evidently did. She figured she was a little more stranded than he was. He at least had his own room and his own clothes. Which reminded her that she was already imposing on his hospitality and she was able to summon a half smile. "Did you hear anything on television?"

"The hurricane is all they're talking about." Jack's gaze swung toward the sliding doors. Outside, the wind plastered an empty chip bag to the glass. Debris littered the balcony. "The weatherman is hemming and hawing like crazy. Looks like we're getting the tail end of Bonnie after all."

"It was supposed to miss us. We were only going to get a little backlash." She massaged the back of her neck and briefly closed her eyes. When she opened them again, he was watching her.

He had moved a little closer, or maybe she imagined it. The smile was gone from his face. His eyes were trained on hers, his gaze steady and piercing. "I'm sorry about your trip to Honolulu," he said.

She shrugged and shuffled a few steps away. "I haven't given up yet. Sometimes these tropical storms blow over quickly."

His grin was faint and sympathetic, and she knew he didn't believe that would happen any more than she did.

She sighed. "Maybe they did cancel the auditions."

"I'm sure of it." Nodding as he reassured her, his voice was deep and hypnotic. The groove in his cheek deepened. "In the meantime, put your feet up, order room service, get comfortable…whatever you want…"

Eyes crinkling at the corners, he gestured toward the bed.

Dani blinked, swallowed. She took a deep breath. In all fairness, he hadn't really singled out the bed. He'd merely swept his hand over the room. But it wasn't that large a room. And the bed just happened to be in the middle of it. She took another breath.

"I'm going to the front desk," she said and swiveled toward the door.

"There aren't any rooms left, if that's what you're thinking."

"How do you know?"

"Because they were sold out when I booked mine a month ago."

"But you got one," she countered with a lift of her chin.

"I'm the groom."

Any momentary smugness she'd felt at undermining his argument was sucked from her like water in a whirlpool.

"Yes, you are," she said, and hurried out before he could say another word.

"NOT EVEN A PARLOR?" Dani asked, her elbow propped on the counter, her chin sinking into the palm of her hand.

"Not even a closet," the front desk clerk assured her with a somber shake of his head. "We don't even know what'll happen to the staff who are stuck here, too."

She brightened. "That's right. You have to do something with them."

"So far it's the ballroom floor for us tonight."

She eyed the man's name tag, then smiled. "Look, Kimo, how about—"

"Sorry." He cut her off with a flash of white teeth against his brown face. "I can't make any deals. I'm just filling in."

She pursed her lips as he turned to answer a question from another guest. Where the heck was the aloha spirit the islands were famous for? she thought grouchily as she dislodged her chin from her palm and turned to idly survey the busy lobby.

The normally sedate and well-appointed area was bustling with bright flowered shirts and even brighter dresses. People huddled together in clusters on the sofas and chairs, chattering, frowning, peering anxiously out at the savage ocean. Tension hummed above the notes of the piano player, who persisted with forced cheer near the lobby bar.

At the end of the counter, a couple was having an all-out war. The poor clerk behind the counter stood speechless, her eyes widening in alarm. The blond woman causing the commotion was about Dani's age, maybe a little younger, and considerably better dressed than her companion. She looked annoyed enough to deck him. Dani hoped they weren't newlyweds.

Kimo was free again and when she turned back to ask him something, she found him watching the couple, too.

He switched his attention to her and, flashing another megawatt smile, he said, "The Brewster bride's sister."

Dani frowned. It was an odd thing for him to say. There was no way she could be linked to the wedding. Unless he knew about Jack. And her. And the baby.

Cautiously she eyed him. His grin widened. She

cringed, her initial question shriveling up and drowning in humiliation. But as the couple wandered off toward the elevators, Dani couldn't help but follow the blonde with her gaze. The woman was rather stunning and that made Dani wonder about her sister, Jack's fiancée.

Melancholy stole a path up her spine, splayed at the base of her skull and delivered a king-size ache to her temples. Pushing away from the counter, she glanced helplessly at Kimo.

"Want an aspirin?" he asked.

She straightened. Who *was* this guy? "No, thanks."

It was stupid, she knew. Absolutely impossible that this guy could read her mind, but she carefully kept her thoughts off Jack and his bride and his bride's sister as she skulked away from the counter and headed across the lobby.

Her self-control lasted all of one minute. It didn't help that smack-dab in front of her was the bickering couple still waiting for an elevator.

Her steps faltering, Dani quickly averted her eyes. She had no desire to come face-to-face with any member of the bride's family. Guilt and embarrassment made it easy to slow her pace as her gaze darted in search of a stairwell.

Guilt? Where did that come from? Stunned that she suddenly felt like the "other woman," she mentally shook herself. She hadn't done anything wrong. She'd merely done a job she'd been paid to do. It wasn't as if she'd asked to be stranded.

Straightening her shoulders, she stepped up beside the couple and calmly waited for the elevator.

You feel guilty because you're attracted to Jack, a tiny voice prodded her.

Ridiculous.

Shifting uneasily, she crossed, then uncrossed her arms. And was promptly reminded that she was wearing Jack's jersey. She quickly recrossed her arms as if to hide that fact, and sneaked a peek at the blond woman.

Dani didn't have to worry about the woman paying her any attention. She was way too busy being irritated by her handsome companion. He was smirking. She looked spitting mad. Or she would have if she didn't have a natural and casual elegance about her that Dani envied all the way down to her own sock-covered toes.

Jack's socks, she reminded herself, and shuffled a foot away. She wondered again about his fiancée. And whether she was anything like her beautiful sister.

She sighed too loudly, and the couple turned to glance at her. Smiling faintly, she unnecessarily pushed the lighted elevator button, grateful that at least they didn't know who she was or that she had any connection to Jack.

"Ms. Carpenter?"

Dani turned at the sound of her name. And so did Stephanie's sister. Kimo was hurrying across the lobby toward her, holding something up in his hand.

"I'm glad I caught you," he said when he got within a few feet. "Mr. Keaton just called down. He asked me to give you his key."

JACK GRINNED when he heard the knock at the door. It had to be Rik. Pleading with his friend on the phone for the past five minutes must have paid off—Rik was coming to the rescue.

He muted the television sound and opened the door. The smile fled from his face.

"Are you crazy?" Dani stood in the corridor, her

cheeks flaming red, her eyes stormier than the sky out-side. She marched forward, her hands up as if to warn him off, and he swiftly backed up.

"What?" He had to duck to the right to avoid being run over.

She rushed past him into the room, then swung around to face him, hands on her hips.

"What?" he repeated, this time in a lower voice, hoping not to wake Sam. He eased the door closed with barely a click.

She held up a hotel key card. "Really smooth move, Jack."

"Good. Kimo caught you." He frowned. "Why didn't you use it?"

"Yeah, Kimo caught me all right. In front of the elevator, where there were a gazillion people—including your sister-in-law to be."

"Bentley?" He smiled. He'd always liked Stepha-nie's sister. She had a lot of spunk. They'd had great times together as kids.

"Jack? Are you listening to me?"

"Sure. Bentley's here already, huh?"

Dani let out a low throaty sigh of disgust.

He put a silencing finger to his lips and glanced at Sam. "Was she with anyone?"

"Jack." She advanced until her face was a scant six inches from his. Her eyes glowed a brilliant green, the rosiness in her cheeks accenting them, making the color all the more spectacular. "Pay attention." Her warm breath clipped his chin. "Your fiancée's sister saw him give me *your* key."

"Huh?" He watched the corner of her mouth twitch, her lower lip quiver in reaction. "Oh, that's okay. Bentley probably knows about us."

"Us?"

"Steph and me."

Her eyes grew wider and she opened her mouth. Although he didn't understand why, her temper was clearly at the boiling point.

He briefly glanced at Sam again, then Jack covered her mouth with his hand. He felt her hot breath skim his palm, heard her suck it back in. She went perfectly still. She blinked once. Twice.

Warm soft lips moved beneath his hand, and with instant clarity he knew why she was upset. Why he should be upset, too.

Heat shot up his arm, across his chest, down his stomach and pooled in his groin. Oxygen swirled overhead just out of reach.

Abruptly, he withdrew his hand and stepped back.

Lightning flashed outside while silence crackled inside. Her accusing look bridged the narrow gap between them.

"Sam." He offered the explanation with a shrug, the single word sounding lame even to him.

Her expression softened as she slid a look at the baby. "I wasn't going to shout." She turned back to Jack, the edginess returning to her face. "I just don't think you're taking this seriously enough."

"I am. Was anyone with Bentley?"

"Yes. A man. I assumed he was her husband."

"But her mother wasn't there, was she?" he asked, a little worried now.

Frustration clouded her eyes. "Who knows? Maybe." Rubbing her hands together, she prowled the room. "I only know what the clerk told me. This is getting very complicated."

"Look. The baby is the only complicated part. We…you and I…didn't do anything wrong."

She spun toward him, her gaze locking with his. The word *yet* hung silently between them.

"The employees are sleeping in the ballroom," she said after a moment. "I'll speak to the manager about stashing my things in an office and then I—"

"There's no need to act hastily," he insisted. "If Bentley did hear anything, she won't repeat it. Like I said, she understands. It's the rest of the family I'm worried about. We'll just have to lay low. I don't want to embarrass Stephanie."

"*We* aren't laying anywhere." She briefly closed her eyes in dismay when she realized how that sounded. "How can Bentley understand? *I* don't understand."

Jack massaged the growing tension in his neck. Hell, he didn't understand much of anything anymore either. He couldn't very well tell Dani that this wedding was a sham, that he was sorry he'd agreed to marry Steph. He couldn't tell anyone. Even Rik only knew part of it.

"After I explain everything, Stephanie is going to appreciate the fact that you're helping me out with Sam. She won't be the problem. It's her mom."

She stared back, skepticism and curiosity evident in the furrow of her brow. Crossing her arms, she hugged herself, looking like she wanted to believe him, looking a little afraid to do so.

For an insane moment, he had an overwhelming urge to tell her everything. He wanted to ease her mind. He wanted to unburden his conscience. It would be easy to do. She seemed so familiar to him. But that was crazy. He'd only met her a couple of hours ago.

Yet the inconceivable pull to spill his guts was there,

reeling him in like a well-hooked marlin. Maybe it was his old football jersey that swallowed her slender body, and brought him fond memories of another lifetime. Or maybe the illusion of security was created by the fact that she was accepting enough not to demand answers.

Except she was, after all, a stranger, one who had brought him nothing but trouble dusted with talcum powder.

"Stay," he said simply.

She unfolded her arms, and they fell awkwardly to her sides. Clenching one hand, she dragged the other down the front of her thigh. "Well, I guess we can at least discuss this—this problem like reasonable adults."

"Right." He started to take her hand, thought better of it, and gestured her toward the small couch. "Let's be logical about this."

"That's the problem. I'm a very logical person. Usually." Frowning, she took a seat, jerkily curling her smooth tanned legs beneath her. They were well shaped and firm. They looked like a dancer's legs. "It must be the storm. It's throwing me off course."

He tried not to smile as he sank into an adjacent chair, absurdly pleased that he wasn't alone in this befuddled state. "Did you find out anything at the front desk about the weather?"

"Nothing other than it's going to get worse before it gets better. The good news is that they haven't closed the airport, though a lot of good that does either of us with the road washed out."

"I haven't been able to get through to Stephanie yet. I still don't know if she can leave Honolulu."

"You called?"

"Yeah, I called." He wasn't that much of a heel.

He cared about his fiancée. He just wished he didn't have to marry her.

"Don't sound so defensive. I just wanted to know if the outside lines were working."

"They're working, but it's still hard to get one."

He noticed that her gaze kept straying to the glass doors. Snack wrappers swirled in miniature whirlwinds, latching briefly to the trees, then bursting into oblivion.

He thought about closing the drapes. They didn't need to watch the show to understand the havoc being created by the wind. It hissed through window seams and rattled the glass. When Dani jumped at a particular nasty assault, he did end up drawing the drapes.

"Okay," he said, returning to his seat, "let's figure out what we're going to do." She nodded, and he continued, "The concierge isn't back yet. No one seems to know where she is. How long did she have Sam before you picked him up?"

"I don't know."

"So we can't assume that his mother is stranded at the hotel, too." He paused when she frowned. "What?"

"Are you sure you have no idea whose baby this is?"

The suspicion in her voice irritated him. "How could you ask me that?"

"It's just that his mother must be terribly frantic by now...unless you're really..."

"I don't have a son, Dani, and if I did, I would never have abandoned him." He felt unjustifiably wounded. This woman didn't know him. Not that he should care what she thought anyway. He tensed, waiting for her reaction.

She didn't look at all contrite for having voiced her

renewed misgiving. She simply stared back as if measuring his sincerity. Yet what did she have to go on? It wasn't as if he'd played the part of the heartbroken groom. He wouldn't be surprised if he came up short in her estimation.

"I believe you," she said, her lips curving slightly before thinning again. "Which means the mother may be having second thoughts and trying to call you right now."

"Good point." He exhaled. "Another reason for sticking close to the room."

"Which brings us back to our problem."

She'd said *our problem*. This was a good sign, except that they had both managed to avoid the subject they'd needed to discuss in the first place. "I can't very well go traipsing around the hotel with a baby. Besides not wanting to run into Stephanie's parents, I don't know who all her friends are, but they could very well pick me out. So I either stay confined to quarters with Sam, or when I need to go out—"

"That's where I come in."

"I'll pay you for your time."

"That isn't necessary." She chewed at her lower lip. "Nor is it the point."

"You do need a place to stay. And no one has to know you're here."

"Are you forgetting about the key incident?"

"I'll square it with Bentley, if need be."

She sent him a quizzical look. He knew she had questions. Ones he couldn't answer.

"I give you my word it will be okay with Stephanie."

"Well, I guess it won't kill me to stick around." She glanced at the Mickey Mouse watch on her wrist, then her gaze drifted lower to the gray shorts that hit her a couple of inches above the knee.

His gaze floated lower still, to the golden expanse of well-toned leg that made his shabby running shorts seem like a piece of art. When she cleared her throat he returned his attention to her face.

"Did I thank you for lending me these clothes?" She pinched the hem of the shorts and held it out. The fabric rode up several inches higher, and his gaze again riveted to her legs.

He almost told her that was thanks enough, but he didn't think she'd appreciate the humor. "No problem. Now, about tonight—"

"I'll check with the manager."

She still didn't get it, he realized, and it took him a split second to decide how to handle the situation.

Pretending he hadn't heard her, he asked, "Which side of the bed do you want?"

Chapter Five

Dani stared silently at him, her eyes widening, her jaw growing slack. Her head tilted slightly to the side. Then she straightened and smiled, as if she'd worked out her problem. "I'm sorry. I didn't hear you correctly."

He grinned back. "What side of the bed do you usually sleep on? I'm pretty flexible."

Hands clenching, she fisted the baggy shorts causing them to ride up high on her thigh. "I'm not *sleeping* here."

He tore his gaze away from her smooth golden skin and knew he should renege right now. He could pretend that he was kidding or that she'd misunderstood. Asking her to stay the night was out-and-out asking for trouble.

He forced his attention to a neutral point on her chin. "I thought we just settled that."

"I said I'd stay and help with Sam. I only meant for the rest of the day...not the entire night."

"You'd rather sleep in the ballroom with a bunch of strangers?"

She gave him a funny look. "You're a stranger, too, Jack."

"Not really." He stopped, and while watching the

small smile that started to curve her lips, the slight and familiar overlap of her front teeth, he mentally calculated how much time had passed since she'd appeared at his door. It seemed like weeks ago. But in fact, it had only been a few hours.

Jumping to his feet, he headed for the small bar. "Look, you want a Coke or a beer or something?"

"Any soft drink without caffeine."

He shuffled the contents of the fridge. "The only diet drinks we have are full-leaded colas."

"None of that diet stuff. I need a clear head. Give me something with sugar."

Chuckling, he pulled out a 7UP for her and a beer for himself. As soon as he handed her the can, she glanced pointedly at her watch.

"Now, we've managed to waste two minutes, and we still haven't solved our problem," she said, then looked up at him.

He dramatically grasped his chest. "Good aim. But I wasn't stalling. I really was thirsty." He uncapped his beer and took a long pull. "Now, what's this business about me being a stranger?" He gave her his most charming smile.

She returned a respectably good dirty look. "Not only are you a stranger, you are one who is about to be married."

When she started to flip the tab on her can, Jack automatically reached for it. But unlike Stephanie, Dani's nails were short, blunt and sensible and she popped the can open in a second.

"Okay," he said, "I understand how you might feel uncomfortable. What can I do to reassure you?"

"Ask me again in about a year?"

He laughed. "To spend the night?"

She laughed, too. "That didn't come out right, did it?" Sobering, she shook her head. "I'll stay for a few more hours and you'll be free to scout around the hotel. Maybe you'll find the concierge. Then I'm sure you can handle Sam by yourself for one night. In the meantime, let's hope the mother contacts you."

Jack could tell by the way she furrowed her brow in concentration that she'd thought seriously about this and that she was set on this solution. So he had no choice but to pull out all the stops.

"Yeah, okay," he said, thoughtfully rubbing his chin. "That sounds reasonable. If I can't find the concierge, I'll contact the manager."

"That won't do any good. Other than get that poor woman fired."

"He'll make sure I get an outside line."

She frowned. "Why?"

"To call Social Services. I'll have to turn Sam over to them."

Her mouth dropped open in outrage. "You can't do that."

He shrugged. "I don't have much choice."

"Of course you do. You wait for his mother to contact you." She jumped to her feet and hurried over to the basket Sam was delivered in. After rooting through it a moment, she turned back to him. "We still have a few diapers and when we run out we'll get what we need from the gift shop. As far as his formula goes..." She frowned. "You know his mother really couldn't have planned on leaving him here for long because she would have left an extra bottle. Oh—here's two cans of powdered stuff. I wonder how much *that* makes."

Her forehead creased in worry, she glanced down at the still peacefully sleeping baby. Immediately her expression softened and she turned sad eyes to Jack. "You can't turn him over to just anyone."

Hell. He was almost sorry he'd used that ploy to get her to change her mind. Her lips turned down at the corners, censure dimming her green eyes and he could tell that she was disappointed in him.

"Running out of formula is going to be a real problem," he protested in his defense.

"Yeah, but if you call Social Services, they won't be able to get here anyway," she said, the thought brightening her mood.

"So what do you suggest?"

"We wait for the mother or the concierge—whoever calls first."

"And in the meantime?" He didn't bother mentioning that they were right back to where they'd started.

"We talk."

"Talk?"

Gently she removed the pacifier that had slipped out of Sam's mouth and laid it to the side, before reclaiming her seat and locking her gaze on Jack. "You know—get to know each other."

His heart slid to his stomach. He hated when women wanted to *talk.* They didn't know the meaning of the word. Talking meant finding out who won the last hockey game, or whether the Cowboys would make it to the Super Bowl again. Rik could vouch for that.

But women wanted more. They wanted you to lay your guts out so that they could analyze the hell out of them. Then tell you that you were still holding back. Damn, the last time he'd agreed to talk to a woman, he ended up saying he'd marry her.

"Talk?" he repeated warily.

She smiled. A very determined smile.

He sprawled out farther in the chair, hoping to exude confidence while his brain scrambled for a way out of this mess. She waited expectantly, one eyebrow beginning to arch. Muttering to himself, he rubbed his tired eyes. He supposed he deserved this for pulling the Social Services stunt.

"Okay, what do you want to talk about?" he asked slowly.

"Anything. Everything. You go first."

He slouched in his seat. Here it came. She wanted him to spill the beans about his upcoming marriage, about how he'd made a mistake in agreeing to Stephanie's plan.

"I'm not clear on this," he hedged. "Maybe you should go first."

"You'd like me to set the tone?" she asked sweetly.

The shrewd gleam in her eyes gave her away. This was a trick question. He took two more gulps of his beer, then grinned. "Hey, if you want us to get to know each other, we could play strip poker instead."

The gleam blazed to murderous intent.

"Only kidding." He took another quick swig. "When you say talk, do you mean like who I think will win the San Francisco-Miami game this fall?"

"You're not getting in the spirit of this, Jack."

"What do you want me to do? Confess some deep dark secret?"

"Well, you know, after tomorrow we'll never see each other again. So that might be kind of fun." Her eyes brightened, and he belatedly realized that if she hadn't considered the notion of swapping secrets before, he'd just given her food for thought.

Either that, or she was looking forward to never seeing him again. He drained his beer.

"Thinking you'll get out of here by tomorrow may be too optimistic." He inclined his head toward the drawn drapes, which provided only a modicum of assurance. Despite the locked glass door behind them, a determined wind seeped through the seal and rippled the edges of the fabric, its howl echoing past the barrier, reminding them of the battle being waged outside.

"Optimism doesn't cost a thing. On the other hand, worry causes frowns which cause wrinkles."

Her complexion was flawless, smooth, creamy-looking. Looking at it made him itch to run a thumb down her cheek to feel the softness for himself. She obviously didn't have to worry about wrinkles for a long time. "You must be a very optimistic person," he said.

She accepted the compliment with a wry lift of her lips. "Nice try. But I won't let you change the subject."

"Not me. I'll play the game. It sounds like fun. Kind of like having quick, hot, anonymous sex."

She folded her arms. His jersey tightened across her chest.

He tipped the bottle to his lips. It was empty. "You know what I mean. Haven't you ever wanted to have fast—"

"No."

"Okay, bad analogy." He sighed and got up, taking his empty bottle with him. "You want something else while I'm up?"

She shook her head. "All right, we're off to a start. Now you know I'm an optimistic person, and I know you like indiscriminate sex."

"I do not like indiscriminate sex." His hand froze over a fresh beer and he turned to glare at her. She looked as though she wanted to laugh. Grabbing a Coke, he returned to his chair.

"You just said—"

"I was talking about when I was younger."

"Oh..." she drawled, nodding sagely.

"What does *oh* mean?"

"Well, the fact that you did something when you were younger that you can't do now tells me that—"

"Can't? What do you mean by can't? And that doesn't tell you jack—" He slammed his Coke down on a side table and raked a hand through his hair. He knew this was going to be trouble. He should call the manager himself and get her a damn place for the night.

Dani couldn't hold back her laughter another second. As much as she liked watching him squirm, and as much as it served him right for threatening Sam with Social Services, she could no longer keep a straight face.

She dabbed at the tears of mirth beginning to well in her eyes.

"You're a cheap date," he said after a moment of eyeing her with ill-concealed irritation. Then his mouth twitched. "You're not very experienced with men, are you?"

All her self-control couldn't chase away the giggles as fast as this one question had. She gathered the large jersey around her, wishing she could drown in the folds. She didn't want to play this game anymore. "What do you mean?"

"Darlin', never hit a man below the ego." He winked. "You'll get more trouble than you'll know what to do with."

Starting to relax again, she grinned broadly. "Really?"

"Really." The word was barely out of his mouth when a nasty gust of wind slammed against the building, rattling the entire structure. A strange and wild glimmer sparked in his eyes and he was off the chair in a flash.

Fear sliced through her and she flew across the small couch, but he grabbed her arm and pulled her up to him.

"You don't want to do this, Jack," she whispered.

Behind her a loud crash spurred her deeper into his arms. She hid her face at the side of his neck for a moment while she caught her breath. Then she pulled back, catching the flicker of hurt in his eyes before she turned around.

A large picture of a Hawaiian sunset that had been on the wall above her head now lay on the couch, the glass shattered. Tiny cracks fanned out like a lacy spiderweb through the bright orange sun.

Jack hooked a finger under her chin and brought her face around to his. "Are you okay?"

One of her arms was still locked around his neck. The other lay on his chest, her palm cupping his shoulder—not cupping exactly, more like a death grip. She relaxed her hand. It slid away from him and down to her side.

Moistening her lips, she raised her lashes. He was close. So close she could see tiny specks of gold in his brown eyes. "I'm fine. But I'm sorry I thought that you…"

She tried to step back but he kept his arm clamped around her waist. The tips of her breasts grazed his chest. She sucked in a breath and her nipples pressed more urgently against him.

"Don't worry about it." After a thorough search of her face, his gaze slid to her mouth.

His skin felt warm beneath her fingers and she realized that her other hand still cupped his neck. She opened her mouth to speak, unsure as to what she was going to say, when Sam let out a bloodcurdling scream.

They jumped apart on cue and both hurried over to the bed. Jack reached the baby first and scooped him up.

Sam was trying to catch his breath, hiccuping and crying at the same time. He quieted a little once he was cocooned in Jack's arms, his tiny flailing fists starting to droop.

"He's okay," Jack said, once he'd looked him over and transferred him to his shoulder. "The crash probably startled him out of his sleep."

"Are you sure?" She searched his blotchy, tear-stained face looking for anything amiss.

"Euw! And that's not all that got startled out of the little guy." He held the baby away from him. Sam hiccuped once more, then bestowed his toothless grin on them.

"I'll get the diaper. You change him." She hustled around to the basket.

"Hey, you wanted to talk. Let's talk about this."

"No, thanks."

"I'll flip you for it."

She tossed him the clean diaper. "I'm going to get this picture out of the way before the glass gets dislodged and falls into the carpet."

"Chicken."

"You got it."

She immediately set to work gathering the fallen picture while Jack grumbled under his breath all the way to the bathroom. As soon as she heard the water running, she gingerly set the picture to the side and collapsed on the couch, surprised that her knees had held out this long.

This was an impossible situation. Spending an afternoon with Jack was bad enough, she couldn't imagine staying the entire night.

The insistent wind roared through the trees, sending the hapless coconut fronds splattering against the glass. It didn't help much that Dani couldn't see the assault. Knowing it was happening was scary enough.

Just like her attraction to Jack.

She couldn't see it, couldn't pinpoint anything about him that was compelling her. But the pull was there nevertheless.

And just like the wind, if it gained momentum, this insane temptation would inevitably lead to destruction.

She shivered as a new gust attacked the hotel. If she concentrated, she knew she could think of things she didn't like about Jack. Like his cavalier attitude toward the postponement of his wedding, or his lack of concern for his fiancée.

She knew that assessment was a little unfair. It wasn't that Jack was unconcerned about Stephanie. It was just that Dani knew if she ever fell in love, she'd be crazy with worry if her lover were in this situation, stranded, forced to be away from her. She'd be so worried, she'd be a breeding ground for wrinkles.

The bathroom door was partially open and she could hear Jack cooing to their tiny ward, heard Sam gurgling happily in response.

She took a deep cleansing breath. There was a lot she liked about Jack, too. Like the way he handled Sam. It was obvious he'd had little exposure to babies, yet he jumped in with both feet, assuming responsibility for the little tyke's care and worrying about whether he had enough supplies.

He had a protective streak, too. She hadn't missed the sporadic peeks he'd slid the baby while he slept, the little reassuring pats he generously doled out.

Her chest tightened with the knowledge that he was going to be a great father someday.

To Stephanie's children.

"We're all squeaky clean." Jack and Sam emerged from the bathroom, one grinning, the other looking relieved.

Dani reached for the picture. She'd accomplished nothing but depress herself while they were washing up. And for absolutely no reason. She was exactly where she wanted to be in life. A free spirit, no longer a slave to routine, deadlines, a boring job. She was on the threshold of travel and adventure. She was on top of the world, wasn't she?

Her hand slipped and grazed the shattered glass. A tiny sliver embedded itself in her finger and made her wince.

"Be careful." Jack hunkered down, balancing Sam in one arm, and drew her hand for his inspection. "Don't move until we get this splinter out or it might go deeper."

She yanked back her hand. "Don't worry about it. You take care of Sam."

Jack frowned, staring at her for a moment. Then he rose, and after delivering a couple of successful tickles to Sam's chubby feet, he gave him his pacifier and placed him in the nest of pillows.

When he returned to Dani's side, his expression brooked no argument. "Let me see that finger," he said, crowding her on the small couch, and making no apology.

She made a show of sliding over to give him room, but he ignored her and soaked up her space, her oxygen—her good sense.

Forcing her attention on the small bloody spot on her finger, she tried not to think about how close he was. How his thigh pressed against hers, how his breath danced across her cheek, how his musky scent made the hair lift on the back of her neck.

"You're making too big a deal out of this," she said, trying to scoot away. But she was crammed back against the sofa cushions as far as she could go, and he apparently had no plans of going anywhere.

"You're worse than Sam. Give me your hand."

She had the incredibly childish urge to stuff her hand behind her back, but when she finally looked up and met his velvety brown eyes only inches from her own, all she could do was give him a faint smile along with her injured hand.

He took his time removing his gaze from hers, and gently laid the back of her hand across his other palm. His skin was rough and callused and it was obvious he worked outdoors. But his touch was gentle and soothing. His fingers brushed her wrist and she suddenly realized that her pulse was out of control and that he must surely feel the tension humming through her veins.

She jerked away and started to stand.

"What the devil is wrong with you?" He clamped down hard on her wrist and stopped her from rising.

"The storm," she lied. "It's making me edgy."

"You're going to be a whole lot edgier if you don't

get this piece of glass out. Can you stay still for one minute?''

"No."

He laughed. "Can I bribe you with room service?"

Testing his hold, she rotated her wrist. He wasn't going to budge. "Maybe."

"Be good, let me play doctor, and then I'll place an order."

"You're too old to be playing doctor." She gave one more tug and earned herself a cross look.

"Wrong. It's more fun when you're older." He pinched her bare thigh.

"Ouch!" Surprised, she quit struggling. While she glared at him, he plucked the glass from her finger.

"There you go." He disposed of the sliver in an ashtray, then turned back to dab at the minuscule drops of blood.

"Gee, thanks. Now all I'll have is a bruise." This time she successfully snatched back her hand and stared sullenly at it, while rubbing her thigh with the other.

"Dani, Dani, Dani." He shook his head. "I would never have guessed you could be such a big baby."

"I am not." The idea was laughable. With two brothers whose lives constantly needed mending, and a mother who hadn't quite figured out that she lived on planet Earth, Dani had always been the family rock. "You made the big deal out of this. Not me."

"Sam's far better behaved."

"Yeah? Try taking away his pacifier." She stood up and he followed her.

Amusement lighted up his eyes, sparking a wicked mischievous gleam. He blinked, and the light was gone, replaced by something darker, more intense. "Is that what you need?"

She caught her breath. His intent was clear in the way he moved his face toward hers, in the way his gaze tarried at her lips.

She swallowed. "I really think you bruised me," she said, her voice sounding shallow, breathless. Ducking, she busied herself with needlessly probing her thigh.

"I'm sorry, Dani," he said, and got down on one knee. Before she knew what he was up to, he pressed his lips to the spot she was rubbing.

"Is that better?" he asked, as he slowly slid back up, his body intimately grazing hers.

Chapter Six

Jack felt like he had that time when he'd been rafting down the Amazon and he'd lost both oars. It had rained all night the day before and the water was gushing down like a son of a bitch. He'd lost all control, spinning helplessly in the water, not knowing in which direction he was headed—toward the safety of the shore or the rocky cliff ahead.

But this time was different. This time he'd had control. He'd simply chosen to relinquish it. He'd chosen to head for the cliffs.

Reluctantly, he faced Dani. She looked stunned, her eyes darkening in alarm. He tried to feel guilty, to feel some regret. But the silky texture of her skin remained on his lips and the remorse wouldn't come. It hovered in the recesses of his conscience, edged out by a desire so strong that he had to take a step back.

This was crazy. Not only did he not know this woman, but he was about to be married. To someone else. And here he was, messing with Dani, who was probably one second away from slapping him across the face, if he were lucky and didn't get kneed instead.

"I think it's gone," she said and flipped her ponytail

away from her pink-tinged cheeks. He must have frowned, because she added, "The bruise? It's gone."

"Oh, good." He rubbed his jaw, and realized that he hadn't shaved yet today. His eyes automatically went to the area he'd kissed on her thigh to check for a whisker burn. When he raised his gaze, he saw the panic in hers. "Look, Dani—"

"Don't." She held up a hand and sidestepped him.

"I just want to apologize."

She threw him a wary sidelong glance. "That's not necessary."

She was lying, he thought, as he watched her stiffly turn to check on Sam. She did want an apology, or maybe not an apology but something that would erase the tension he'd caused by his foolish impulsiveness.

"Dani, I'm sorry. I had no right touching you."

"I know. And I..." Pressing her lips together, she stared down at her hands. They stilled for a moment, in the middle of plumping the baby's pillows, then just as swiftly they returned to rearranging and fluffing where none was needed.

Sam obviously thought it was a game she was playing and started punching at her, laughing and gurgling as he sliced awkwardly into the air between them. That brought a smile to her lips, and as grateful for that as Jack was, he felt like a jerk all over again for having caused her distress in the first place.

"Do you want a Band-Aid for your finger?" he asked, hoping he hadn't totally blown it and that she was still speaking to him.

"No, it's fine." She did give him a half smile.

"Can I do anything for you?"

She stayed silent for nearly a minute, her expression indecisive as she studied him. "Yes, you can."

He released a breath. "Name it. Anything."

"Call Stephanie."

"What?" He shook his head in confusion.

"Trust me on this. She wants to hear from you. Even if the news hasn't changed."

Hell. She thought he was a bigger jerk than he actually was. "I already tried calling her. Besides, like I've told you, she's a very capable woman."

"Well, try again." She paced several steps, her movements jerky, agitated. "And keep trying until you get her."

He didn't want to call Stephanie from the room. It was bound to be an awkward conversation with Dani there. And he certainly didn't want to ask her to leave. Especially not now.

He briefly considered explaining the situation to his fiancée. He could do that in front of Dani, but then Steph would worry about whether her mother was there and if she'd seen the baby and what kind of scandal it would cause. And Stephanie feared Babs Brewster a lot more than she did a mere hurricane. Wasn't that why he was in this mess?

"Why do *you* want me to call her, anyway?"

"Because no matter how capable she is, she needs to know you care," she said, coloring slightly, and he suspected that she wasn't telling him everything that was on her mind.

"She knows that." He moved to the window and pushed aside the drapes. Not because he wanted to watch the gray, angry waves mercilessly pound the shore, but because he didn't understand what was going on here, and it was damn frustrating.

After a moment of letting the thoughts spin in his head, he figured he got it. Releasing the drapes, he turned to look at her and knew for sure by the disappointment mirrored in her eyes.

And with an alarming ache in his chest, he also knew that while his estimation of her had just risen a notch, her opinion of him had plummeted two.

"I think it's noble of you to empathize with my fiancée, but I assure you it's unnecessary." He left the window to sort through the things he'd pulled out of his jeans pocket earlier and had dumped on the dresser. Finding his comb, he bent to see his reflection in the mirror and tackled his hair.

It was only mildly disarrayed and he strained to remember if Dani's hands had ever made their way there. Everything had happened so fast. The impetuous kiss, the closeness.

He turned to find her watching him. Her lower lip was drawn slightly under her teeth, and her eyes darkened with such unconscious longing that his hand faltered.

God, he wanted to kiss her again.

"I'll be back in a few minutes," he said as he rushed to the door.

"Where are you going?"

"To do something I should have done in the first place." He hesitated at the open door, not wanting to face the accusation in her eyes when he virtually admitted that he'd deliberately held back the perfect solution. "To find Rik and ask if I can bunk with him."

PEOPLE CROWDED the foyer area outside the elevators. Employees, in the hotel's blue floral uniforms, hustled in and out of clusters of noisy tourists who stood gawking out at the storm. Although what they hoped to see, Jack couldn't guess. The hotel staff had hung enormous sheets of heavy canvas at the end of open-air corridors where the buildings previously had no barrier or obstacle to the ocean view.

The exposed lounge area was blocked off, too. It seemed odd to think that just a few short hours ago it had still been pleasant enough to sit in the bar and feel the tropical breeze. Now the wind whipped off the ocean and battered the canvas protectors, the only thing keeping the storm from pillaging the tropical-weather-friendly hotel.

That didn't seem to stop people, though, from jockeying for positions around the lobby and bar, trying to get a glimpse of the thrashing ocean and the destruction being wreaked by the wind.

It made it hard for Jack to locate Rik. When he hadn't found him in his room, he thought he might find him in the bar. The basketball championship was still being televised around weather bulletins, and he figured Rik had opted to watch the game with other people.

But the noise level was absurd and visibility even more so, and Jack was about to give up when he thought he saw Rik's dark head moving quickly across the lobby. Since he was taller than anyone else, Jack easily kept abreast of him until he got his attention.

"Hey, what are you doing down here? Is the baby okay?" Rik frowned, looking past him as if he were expecting someone.

"Yeah, he's fine. He's with Dani. Look, Rik..."

A grin, slow and hesitant, tugged at his friend's lips.

Jack scratched his chest, stalling, wondering yet dreading what Rik was reacting to. "What?"

"Who's Dani?"

"You met her."

"Yeah, I met her. But who is she? I mean what's going on between you two?"

Jack gave him a suitably appalled look. "Nothing. She's helping me with the baby."

"Out of the goodness of her heart?"

"I'm paying her." He didn't know why he lied, except that the guilt had begun seeping in and he didn't need anyone reading anything more into what was happening than was necessary. Or questioning him about it.

Rik's brows drew together as he contemplated that information. For whatever reason, he didn't look pleased. Which made Jack feel all the guiltier. Here he was talking about another woman to the man who would be best man at his wedding. And as much as Rik might think Jack was making a mistake, he wouldn't expect him to betray Stephanie.

"That's why I've been looking for you," Jack declared.

He put up his hands. "I'm not baby-sitting."

"I wasn't asking. I need to share your room tonight."

"What about your room?"

"Dani's going to stay there with Sam," Jack said, relieved to finally set the record straight.

"So?"

"So, I can't sleep there, too."

"Why not?"

"Are you nuts?"

"Look, drastic situations call for drastic measures. How many times have we said that?"

Jack stared dumbly at his friend. And he was worried what the idiot would think? He slipped an arm around his buddy's shoulders. "Let me explain this slowly—"

Rik shook his head, and cut in. "I can't help you."

Jack responded with a muttered curse. "I only need a place to crash."

Unmoved, Rik glanced over his shoulder. "I think I already have a roommate."

"Who?"

"None of your business."

Rik started to walk away and Jack reached out to nab his shoulder when he saw his future mother-in-law leave the elevator and head his way.

"Son of a..." Jack let Rik go, using his hand to push through his hair instead.

He wasn't through with his friend yet, not by a long shot, but right now he had to get out of here before Babs Brewster spotted him.

Bending at the knees so that he wasn't so easily visible above everyone else, he headed for the outskirts of the lobby and toward the bank of elevators. Babs's hair was stylish and blond and despite her shorter stature, he had an easy time keeping track of her.

He made it within a few feet of an open elevator and exhaled audibly. Babs was about the last person he needed to see. It wasn't that he didn't like her. She had always been fairly decent to him in his rebellious adolescent years. But as gracious, well-bred, old moneyed as she was, she could be a barracuda.

He sidestepped a young couple who were too busy smooching on their way out of the elevator car to see where they were going, when he heard Babs call out his name.

The bell dinged and the doors quivered enticingly on either side of him.

Jack hesitated before turning around. He had one second to plan his strategy.

DANI FLIPPED THROUGH every working television channel three times. Apparently one of the local stations was already down. At any rate, there was only static where the news should have been. This did not look good.

She moved a little closer to Sam, bunching up the pillows behind her and staring past her stockinged feet at the television screen positioned at the far wall.

At least the airport hadn't closed yet, and they hadn't lost power, she told herself. Maybe this was the height of the storm. Maybe in a few hours everything would be back to normal and the hurricane will have stayed on its predicted course—away from the islands.

She smiled and absently patted Sam's bottom. Everyone was probably worrying for nothing.

The lights flickered. Static filled the television screen.

"Oh, hell's bells." She stared up at the ceiling as if she could maintain power by sheer will. After the brief scare, the lights remained on and the television resumed its broadcast.

It had been less than half an hour since Jack left, but already she was restless and edgy. Which was totally ridiculous because she was far better off with him gone.

She flipped through two more channels. No one was saying anything different. This was the worst storm to hit the islands in two decades. So far, the weather bureau still classified it as such. None of the weathermen would stick his neck out and predict it would eventually be labeled a hurricane, but it didn't matter. Dani knew deep in her bones they were in for a bad night.

Or was she getting her signals crossed? Maybe the danger she sensed was more personal. Hurricane Jack had already messed up her day, her weekend—maybe even her life. She should be on her way to Honolulu, not lusting after a soon-to-be-married man. One who treated his upcoming vows with such casual disregard. How could she be attracted to a man like that? To a man who professed to love someone else and still kissed her?

God, but she wanted him to kiss her again. She slumped farther down into the pillows. So what kind of sleazeball did that make her?

He was going to be staying in another room. She'd be alone with Sam for the night. Tomorrow she'd be outta here. No need to panic.

Sam squealed with pleasure at something. He seemed to have a bizarre fascination with his feet and she figured that was the object of his amusement. But when she turned to look at him, he was focused on her.

"You, too, you little hurricane," she said, tickling his tummy. "You see what you've done." He laughed and gurgled, and she tickled some more. "Do you? Huh? Do you?"

She grinned at the unexpected throaty chuckle Sam issued, and they continued to play and laugh until she heard the door click.

Jack looked as though he'd been through the eye of the storm when he stepped into the room and headed straight for the refrigerator.

He stooped down and peered inside. "Beer or chocolate? Pick your poison," was the first thing he said.

She pressed the mute button on the remote. "Both. What happened?"

He nodded, broke an almond chocolate bar in half and handed it to her along with a beer. Grabbing another for himself, he moved to the couch, plopped down and bit a chunk off his half of the candy bar.

"Maybe you ought to unwrap it first," she said.

"Huh? Oh." He made a face and removed the candy from his mouth.

"Did you find Rik?"

"Anything new?" He inclined his head toward the television.

"No," she said with more than a trace of impatience. "What did he say?"

"He can't help us."

"Why not?"

He uncapped his beer and took a sip. "He's got company."

She winced when the newly unwrapped chocolate followed his beer. "Company?"

"Company," he confirmed without looking at her, making her think he was hiding something.

"Company?" she repeated with healthy skepticism.

"Yeah, company." He looked at her then, his gaze dark and meaningful.

"Oooh, company," she said, nodding.

He still looked funny and she knew embarrassment had nothing to do with his demeanor. She half hoped it was because he felt bad about what had happened between them earlier. But then that would sort of make him a nice guy again and she was better off thinking he was a jerk. Besides, nothing physical would happen again. She wouldn't allow it.

"So what happened?" she queried, her curiosity getting the better of her.

"That's it."

"So why do you look like you broke your favorite toy?"

"I saw Stephanie's mother."

"And?"

He slid her a quick look, one dark brow climbing in amusement. Then he made her wait as he polished off his candy bar and licked two fingers.

"I'm not being nosy." She sniffed peevishly. And got a strong whiff of chocolate. The aroma was too much to ignore and she unwrapped her half of the candy bar as she spoke. "Whether I like it or not I'm involved, and I'm not up for any more surprises. What happened after you ran into her?"

"That's not what I said. I didn't run into her." One side of his mouth lifted in a wry curve. "Actually, I saw her. And ran."

"Did she see you?"

"I believe so."

"So you don't think that looked suspicious?"

"The lobby was crowded. She probably thinks I didn't hear her."

"Well, if she called out to you, of course she saw you. Maybe she's even heard from Stephanie," Dani said around her first bite of candy, then stopped munching altogether. "You're a coward, Jack Keaton."

"I've told you already. There are things you don't understand." He refused to meet her gaze and, neglecting his beer, stared moodily off at nothing in particular.

Dani decided she'd butted in enough and didn't say anything more, allowing silence to settle between them.

They sat that way for several minutes until the phone rang, and Jack instantly held up a hand. "Don't answer it."

Of course she wouldn't answer it. She wasn't stupid. Miffed, she watched the parade of emotions cross his face. There was a struggle waging inside him, of that much she was certain. And her pique quickly subsided with the realization that his problem was much more involved than a bad mother-in-law joke.

On the fourth ring, he answered the phone.

After waiting for the caller to identify herself, he said, "Hi, Babs." Then sank wearily back into his seat and closed his eyes. "Actually I was just on my way out, but I thought you might be Stephanie. Have you heard from her?"

Following a brief silence, he said, "That's all I know, too."

He shook his head occasionally, but didn't speak again for quite a while. Finally, he said, "I'm not sure what you expect me to do about the weather, Babs."

Again, silence on his end.

"Okay, okay, I understand. No, I'll have to take a rain check on that drink. I'm late as it is."

He crossed his eyes at Dani while he continued to nod at the phone. The unexpected stab at levity made her smile.

"If I hear from her again, I'll let you know. Of course I will. I really have to go now. I won't forget. Bye, Babs. Yes, goodbye, Babs," he said firmly, already moving the receiver away from his mouth.

He'd scarcely replaced the instrument when he groaned. "That woman never quits."

Only Dani was barely listening. She was stuck on the word *again.* He obviously had already talked with Stephanie. He'd simply chosen not to tell her. Which was perfectly okay. It was none of her business. He was just so damn cryptic it irritated her.

"What's the pout for?" he asked. "At least *you* didn't have to talk to the wicked witch of the north."

"Nice talk."

His shrug was sheepish. "She's always done all right

by me, but she never lets up on Stephanie or Bentley. I spent most of my teen years listening to their complaints and defending them. It's hard to break the habit of knight in shining armor.''

He grinned, but she didn't feel like grinning back. He had just told her more than she wanted to know. And the news was depressing.

A melancholy swiftly descended upon her and she had to mentally shake herself. The feeling was irrational, asinine, totally absurd. She had no right to the emotion. But there it was. Because now she knew that Jack and his fiancée shared a long, memory-filled history, and Stephanie never seemed more real to Dani than she did at this moment. Nor did the painful reminder that Dani was intruding in their lives.

She forced a smile, and said conversationally, "So you two were childhood sweethearts."

"Sort of." His grin faded and that mysterious tone oozed into his voice again.

"And you're just getting married now?"

He lifted a shoulder. "Timing wasn't right before."

"How old are you?"

"Thirty-eight." He rolled his eyes toward the ceiling. "Now you're going to tell me that I obviously have a commitment problem, but I'll save you the trouble and tell you that you're probably right."

She laughed in spite of the sudden blue mood that swamped her. "I wouldn't say that. You *are* getting married, after all."

"Yeah."

There wasn't a trace of joy or enthusiasm on his face. Something close to regret puckered his forehead. He blinked and stared off for a moment, the lines etching deeper between his eyebrows.

And then his expression relaxed and he regarded her with that intense dark gaze of his, his eyes raking her face and missing nothing, and she knew she couldn't hear what he was about to say. If she listened, if she did anything at all but leave, she would forever feel like the other woman.

"I'm sorry, Jack." She moved her arm when he would have laid a hand on her. "I can't stay. I wish there was something I could do to help you out with Sam, but I can't."

He followed her to the door. "Dani, wait."

She fumbled with the knob. "Don't. Please, don't."

He covered her hand with his until she stilled. "You win," he said on a ragged breath. "We need to talk."

Chapter Seven

She was ready to bolt. Jack knew that as well as he knew that she was still wearing his old jersey and that the damn rag had never looked better.

He told himself to let her go. To let her walk out that door so he could get back to business, so that he could keep his word to Stephanie. He'd only known Dani a few hours. She meant nothing to him. There were no ties between them, no bond. She meant absolutely nothing, he told himself again.

Life would be so much simpler if he just let her go.

But the thought of that door closing behind her and possibly never seeing her again zapped him with a jolt of panic so strong that it gave him a chill, and he knew if he let her go now, he would always wonder if he'd made the biggest mistake of his life.

"Give me ten minutes, okay?" He absently stroked the inside of her wrist. And knew immediately that it was a mistake.

She jerked out of his reach. "I haven't got ten minutes."

"I'm afraid you've got all night."

Unappreciative of his little joke, she glared at him, her carriage stiff with censure.

He blew out a weary breath, half-certain he knew what the problem was. And if he were right, he might have to tell her everything. But he'd have to think long and hard before he did that. He'd given his word to Stephanie. "Ten minutes?"

Eyes dark with suspicion and hurt, she inclined her head to the side. "You sit over there."

She stayed where she was, her arms folded across her chest, waiting until he lowered himself into the designated chair. Although not surprised, he had mixed feelings about what she'd just told him by relegating him to the far side of the room—as far away from her as possible.

It pleased him that he apparently affected her as much as she did him, but he also knew that his number was up, that he'd have to tell her about him and Stephanie. He wondered how much of a carrot he could dangle and still keep Dani and his word.

He watched as she sat on the couch, her back straight as a surfboard, her lips pressed as thin as a vanilla wafer. And with a sharp prick to his arrogance, it suddenly occurred to him that she wasn't his to keep, that maybe she had no interest in him at all.

Then he remembered how the silky skin on her inner thigh had begun to pucker under his lips, how she'd automatically pressed her body to his, how her mouth had parted waiting for his kiss.

Hell. He was getting hot all over again.

"I'm waiting," she said, her foot beginning to tap. "And if you don't quit looking at me like that I'll have you moved in with your future mother-in-law."

"Glad you still have a sense of humor," he muttered.

"I'm not kidding."

He supposed she wasn't by the look she was giving him. So much for stalling her. Then the idea hit him. "I forgot that I was supposed to order room service. I'll do that now, okay? Then we'll talk while we wait for it."

"That'll take longer than ten minutes," she said, but she'd hesitated long enough that he knew he could push his advantage.

He also knew that she was hungry because she'd wolfed down her half of the chocolate bar almost as fast as he had demolished his. As she eyed her watch, he said in his best logical tone, "It's dinnertime and we both have to eat."

Quickly, he got up and grabbed the room service menu, then returned to his seat, not wanting to disrupt her sense of security. When he started to read the appetizing entrée descriptions out loud, he knew he had her in the palm of his hand.

"Tell me again what's in the seafood Alfredo," she said after moistening her lips for the second time.

It wasn't hard to tamp down his smugness. He was starving, too. "Let's see…shrimp, crab, clams in a buttery cream sauce—"

"Tell them they have to get it here in, uh, fifteen—"

He wagged a finger. "Remember? You said yourself, you're a very logical person."

"I see you have a long memory," she paused for emphasis, "when it suits you."

He accepted the jab with a wince. She was, of course, referring to his soon-to-be-married status. This was going to be a long evening. "So, you want the Alfredo? How about mango cheesecake for dessert?"

"Do they have macadamia nut cream pie?"

He headed for the phone in order to hide his grin. "Coming up," he said.

"And tell them to bring a to-go bag."

He punched in the extension number, while giving her a give-me-a-break look that she ignored.

"Order some juice for Sam."

"It's already on my list."

"Ask them if they have anything that would be suitable for baby formula."

"I'm one step ahead of you."

"Do babies eat real food at this age?"

He shrugged as the person on the other end of the line answered. After giving the woman their order, he asked what she knew about babies. But she only giggled and even after he assured her he wasn't joking, she was of no help.

"Well, that was unenlightening. How much formula do we have left?" he asked as soon as hung up the phone.

"Two cans of the powdered kind. But who knows how fast he goes through the stuff."

"How about diapers?"

"Enough for tonight, maybe tomorrow."

"I think I ought to run down to the gift shop and see what I can find."

Her eyebrows shot up. "Aren't you forgetting something?"

"Oh, my wallet," he said, patting his empty back pocket, and was pleased to see her gaze linger on the area.

"Don't be obtuse. How long did they say it would take?"

He cringed as he walked to the dresser to get his

wallet. "Remember what a logical, sensible person you are. And there is a storm and it *is* the dinner hour—"

"How long?"

"Haven't I behaved?"

She blinked, and he could tell that his question had caught her off guard. He probably would regret throwing the problem out in the open like this, but he couldn't leave the room, or have her leave and be left to wonder if he'd ever see her again.

"Only recently," she said cautiously.

"You're right. But I'm a new man." He held up both hands in supplication.

"I liked the old one okay," she said, then widened her eyes when she realized how that sounded.

A grin tugged at his lips but he held it in check. "And to prove it to you I'm going to pass on that juicy line you handed me."

She sighed. "I like you, Jack. I think you know that." Her gaze skittered away for a moment, before returning to lock with his. "If I didn't, things would be a whole lot easier. But this—this situation isn't right."

He nodded solemnly. "I understand why you would feel that way."

"How else am I supposed to feel?"

"I wasn't being patronizing." He closed his eyes, wishing he were back in the Amazon. Far away from civilization, from moral obligations, from reminders that you can't always have what you want in life. For a moment, he wished he'd never met Dani. "You may not believe it, but this is hard for me, too."

When he opened his eyes, she was still staring at him. "I know," she said quietly. "We can make this easier if I leave right now."

"That won't solve anything."

"What do you want, Jack? Are you looking for a one-night stand? One last fling before you settle down?"

"No." He was stunned by her sudden flip attitude. "That's not what I want."

Then he saw the hurt in her eyes, and understood what prompted her attack. Fisting his hands, he jammed them into his pockets. Hell, he didn't know what he wanted. Except that he wanted her to stay.

"Good, because I can't help you there."

Her voice had grown small, and he knew that he should tell her about the deal he'd made with Stephanie. Explain right now why he had to go through with this marriage. But that meant betraying Steph. "We can be friends," he said.

"Can we?"

"I can."

Her eyes rounded in alarm and he wondered what the devil he'd said wrong now. Except she wasn't looking at him, but past him, over his shoulder toward the bed.

Her hand fluttered to her breastbone. "But can *he* do *that*?"

Jack turned to see what she was looking at and lunged at the same time she did.

They both reached Sam before he could crawl to the edge of the bed. The baby laughed when Dani scooped him up and swung him into the air.

"Sam?" She was breathless, her voice shaky. "When did you learn how to crawl?"

"Hey, kid, you've been holding out on us." Jack grinned and lightly boxed the child's chin, but he felt pretty shaky himself and his stomach turned again.

She slid him a shy look. "I would have felt awful if—"

"Me, too," he said, cutting her off, not wanting to think about what might have happened while they'd been busy doing the mating dance.

Wrapping her arms around Sam, holding him close for reassurance, she said, "Why don't you go check out the gift shop, and I'll call housekeeping to see if I can get a crib?"

He nodded. "I'll get back here before room service does." With his thumb, he stroked Sam's plump cheek, all puffed out in a toothless grin. "Hey, champ, good thing I ordered you applesauce and not spinach."

Dani smiled and watched Jack leave. Her stomach and pulse rate hadn't quite settled down yet. They'd been lucky so far. Sam had been drowsy and easy to handle, but he'd obviously found his second wind.

Balancing him on one hip, afraid to put him down yet, she punched in the number for housekeeping from the information plate on the telephone.

After five rings no one answered, but she persisted, bouncing Sam on her hip and wondering what the heck she was supposed to do next. A sleeping baby was a piece of cake, but a crawling one would keep Jack on his toes.

So why did she care? This wasn't her problem. She'd already decided she had to leave. A crawling baby shouldn't change that decision. The situation hadn't diminished the strong and unhealthy attraction she felt for Jack.

When Sam started to fuss, she sandwiched the phone between her ear and her shoulder, and swung him up into the air until he started to chortle.

She'd guessed that he was about six or seven months

old and she wasn't really sure what to expect from a baby of that age. Although she had one younger brother, he was only three years behind her so she hadn't been that attentive to his early routines.

Two of her friends had started having kids already, but she'd been too busy with her career to pay much attention. That's when the distance had begun to grow between them. Their priorities had changed and hers had blindly moved forth, until she didn't know whose life she was living anymore. Turning thirty-one last month had proved her own milestone. Now, she was ready for change—adventure.

The phone rang for the fifteenth time. What she was truly ready for was someone to pick up the darn phone. Settling Sam back on her hip, she waited for three more rings, then recradled the receiver in disgust.

Quickly, she picked it up again and tried the hotel operator. And received the same results. Giving up, she took Sam to the bed and lay down beside him. He started kicking and gesturing until his squirming feet caught his attention, and he happily settled down to attack his toes, jibber-jabbering the entire time.

The kid was possessed. What happened to that nice docile baby who had spent the afternoon with them? As cute as he was she didn't know if she should laugh or cry. Sam—this active—was going to be a big problem.

There was a curt, warning knock at the door, and she started to rise when Jack opened it and walked in.

"Oh, it's you." She started to return to her lounging position, then realized what she was doing and sat upright.

That was the problem. She was entirely too comfortable with Jack. As if she'd known him for a long time, and not merely—she glanced at her watch and cringed—six hours.

"You probably have time for a quick nap, if you'd like," he said as he dumped a large package onto the dresser.

"Geez, how long is room service supposed to take?"

"You don't wanna know." He opened the bag and started rooting through it. "But you can't blame them. The staff is going nuts trying to prepare for the storm."

"*Trying to prepare?* Isn't this the storm we're having now?" She shivered involuntarily at the sound of leaves and branches thrashing the building.

"Apparently, it's supposed to get a lot worse."

"Great. Maybe I should head down to housekeeping now instead of waiting until after dinner."

"Didn't you call them?"

"No one answered."

"I'm not surprised." He shook his head and stopped rifling through the bag. "This afternoon they put up canvas panels to protect the lounge off the lobby from the wind. Now they have it totally blocked off. Some of the panels were blown down, the rest are fairly ripped up. The staff is having a hell of a time working against the wind to get them down before they whip off and hurt someone."

Dani worried her lower lip as she considered the import of what he'd just told her. She wondered how her mom was doing, and felt guilty because she hadn't been able to get through to her.

"So a crib won't be on the top of their list," she said finally.

"If they have one I'll go get it and bring it up myself. It can't be that hard for us to set up."

He'd said *us,* she noted. And she didn't miss the

slight emphasis he placed on the word, or the way that he'd hurriedly got back to checking the contents of his bag.

"Did you find some diapers?" she asked.

"Sort of." He pulled out a white T-shirt, then an orange one and another white one with a red scripted slogan.

"I know I'm not an expert here, but I don't think diapers have sleeves in them."

"Don't think of them as sleeves. Consider them wipes." Next he pulled out a pair of scissors.

"Wipes?"

"Yeah, you know when—"

"I know." Or she thought she did, anyway. They sounded rather self-explanatory she figured, as she made sure Sam was reasonably tucked in before leaving his side.

"This is the best I could do. This hotel doesn't exactly cater to babies, or families for that matter. Now, if I needed condoms, I would have had no—"

"Spare me, Jack." She tore one of the T-shirts out of his hands and, noticing that it was an extra-large, wondered if they could get two diapers out of it.

"I wasn't implying anything. Don't be so touchy."

Yeah, right. "You know what we ought to do," she said, frowning at the shirt she was wearing. "We could swap a new shirt for this old jersey."

Pleased with her idea, she glanced up for his approval. His face was a mask of disbelief. His jaw had slackened, his eyes were starting to darken.

Surprised, she reared her head back slightly. "I'm only suggesting it because you'd get a new shirt out of—"

"No way."

"What? You look as though I just asked you to commit murder."

"You might as well have," he grunted, his disbelief sliding to irritation. "Do you know how old that shirt is?"

"Exactly my point."

"If you don't like it, take it off."

Dani glared back, wondering what had got into him. She took no offense at his last crack. He wasn't suggesting anything improper. He'd simply gone nuts. "Fine. We'll cut up the new shirt." Without waiting for him to pass her the scissors, she got a firm grip and tore the neckline. "Makes perfect sense to me."

"You're damn right it does," he mumbled as he handed her the scissors, then pulled a tube of baby oil out of the bag.

Peeved with his churlish behavior, she turned her back on him while she attempted to figure out how best to cut up the shirt. Although she tried to concentrate on what she was doing, her mind kept replaying their odd conversation, and her gaze drew to the old faded jersey she wore.

Upon closer inspection, she noticed that the fabric wasn't like an ordinary shirt, a fact that was easily concealed after so many washings. It was soft and kind of slinky, and the fading in the front was more than just random fading. Something had once been sewn there. Like numbers.

She spun to face him. "Where did you get this shirt?"

His lips stretched into a straight line and he barely spared her a sidelong glance. She could tell he was deciding whether to ignore her, and the thought struck that it was good for her to see this unappealing side to him.

"I think you owe me that simple answer after nearly biting my head off," she said, her free hand on her hip.

He faced her then, his disgruntled look melting to one of contrition, and he was the old Jack again.

"Football," he said with a small shrug.

"I figured that much."

His hands fidgeted, something he wasn't prone to do, and he absently fiddled with the large bulky ring on the finger of his right hand. She realized that she hadn't noticed his class ring before and had the passing thought that he didn't seem the type to wear one—especially one that big and gaudy.

"Did you play in college?" she asked.

"Yeah."

She held the fabric out pinched between her thumb and finger, and grinned. "Then this is *really* old."

He answered with a slow grin of his own. "Now, if *I* had said that to you, I *would* have had my head bitten off."

She laughed. "You're right."

"It's not quite that old, though." He turned back to emptying his bag. "I got it later."

"As in after college?"

"I played pro ball for three years."

"Wow. You're full of surprises." Her gaze returned to his fingers, and her eyes narrowed as she closed the distance between them. "Can I see that ring?"

He held out his hand.

She brought it up close. Her eyes widened as they rose to meet his. "Super Bowl?"

"You got it." He started to return to the task of unloading his purchases.

"I'm not done looking yet." She tugged on his arm until his hand was back in hers. His palm was rough and callused from spending so much time outdoors, and maybe even from throwing a few footballs.

But it was also warm and gentle. She'd seen that in the way he'd cared for Sam.

"When you're not delivering babies, you do palm readings, too?"

"What?" Startled, she looked up to find him studying her with an amused grin. Embarrassed that she'd been unconsciously stroking his palm, she dropped his hand. "Yes, and your lifeline looks awfully short right now."

Chuckling, he left his hand out, palm up. "Anything else?"

"You tell me. Why did you quit playing football?"

He withdrew his hand and used it to rake his hair. "I got hurt."

Her gaze drifted to his denim-covered legs. "Your knee?" She couldn't see anything. She didn't know why she made that assumption.

Annoyance crossed his face and she thought that maybe she'd hit a nerve. "My knee, my back, no one thing in particular. I took a couple of bad hits the year after the Super Bowl." Then he lifted his shoulders in a casual shrug and added, "It happens."

"But that didn't stop you from starting your tour guiding business."

"No. Guiding requires a different type of physical demand."

"You do have your doctor's approval?"

He grinned. "Yes, Mom."

She sighed, slanting him a skeptical frown. "Don't you have to do strenuous things sometimes?"

"Yup, but that's part of life—my life, anyway—the one I've chosen. I damn well won't live it under a rock."

A little rattled, Dani abruptly turned back to fashioning Sam's diaper. If she didn't know any better, she might have thought Jack's brief sermon had been aimed at her.

Chapter Eight

"Just our luck the kid's a night owl." Jack shook his head as he stood over Sam, who curled his small body and happily reached for his feet. "I think he's also double-jointed. Now that he's tired of his thumb and the pacifier, I'll bet you five bucks he gets his toes in his mouth."

Keeping sight of Dani out of the corner of his eye, he noticed that he didn't even get a smile out of her. She just kept stacking their dirty dinner dishes, then she pushed the room service cart near the door.

He had no idea what he'd said wrong, or if he'd done anything at all. She'd been quiet ever since their discussion about his football career, had hardly said a word through dinner. You'd think she was the one who'd got her career cut short, her dream jerked out from under her.

"I thought all kids slept at night, didn't you?" he asked, trying to get her to say something.

"That's wishful thinking." She rolled her eyes toward the ceiling. "I know that much."

"Terrific." This was good. It was a start. "I'm a morning person myself."

Her expression tightened.

Now what? "What about you?" he asked, cautiously.

She picked up a forgotten linen napkin from the end table and threw it on the cart. "Me, too."

"There you go," he said, grinning, "something else we have in common."

She stomped into the bathroom, not looking at all pleased. When she didn't close the door, he caught a glimpse of her straightening her hair at the bathroom mirror. And he knew she was leaving.

"I'll run down to housekeeping now," he quickly called out. "Sam may be more prone to fall asleep if he's in something familiar like a crib."

"I'll do it." She emerged from the bathroom, her hair not looking all that different. Her ponytail was still lopsided. A flurry of dark flyaway tendrils framed her face. She looked great.

"I doubt you'll be able to carry it up by yourself if there's no one to help you," he said, and although that was the truth, he was more concerned with not giving her the opportunity to escape.

The thought staggered him. This wasn't like him to be acting like some crazy, possessive teenager. Part of it was that he didn't know what she was thinking right now. Her sudden moodiness and his not being able to account for it was putting him at odds, and he hated for her to leave on these terms.

"If I can't bring it myself or find someone to help me, then you can go back down and pick it up, okay?" She offered him a smile as if she'd read his thoughts and wanted to reassure him. "But I need to get out of here for a while."

"Sure, I understand." He wanted to ask if it was to

get away from him, but he didn't think he could stomach the answer.

IT WAS BOTH SCARY and exciting to be in the thick of things, Dani thought, as she navigated her way through the lobby. Scary because, with the exception of several landscape spotlights, it was pitch-black outside and while she couldn't see a blessed thing, she could still hear the surf slamming the beach, the wind blasting the building.

Where once you could gaze out over the ocean from the center of the lobby, now large canvas partitions had been tightly stretched from floor to ceiling. Yet even with all the precautions the hotel had employed, it was impossible to block the full furor of the wind. It whizzed through narrow openings and shot tremors of fear up the spines of captivated onlookers if Dani was any gauge, that is. It must be morbid fascination, she figured, that compelled the throngs of people to the lobby when their own rooms were far more sheltered. At least, she assumed irritably, they all had rooms.

Of course morbid fascination had to account for her own growing sense of excitement, too. She'd felt its sting the moment she'd stepped off the elevator, heard the buzz of the crowd, absorbed the hum of tension. The feeling clawed at her nerves and twisted her insides into such a tangle of hope and dread that she wanted to curl into a ball and sleep until the worst was over—whenever the heck that was.

If her mother were here, she'd tell Dani it was some kind of premonition, that something big was surely about to happen. But in all this craziness, there was one small thing for which Dani could be thankful. Her mother wasn't here.

By the time she made it to the front desk, at least seven people were ahead of her in line. The two women behind the counter looked tired and totally stressed out, yet they patiently answered each question.

Dani didn't mind the wait. This time away from Jack was good for her. She didn't want to like the man. She didn't want to have anything in common with him, but it seemed as though, on both accounts, she was constantly being thwarted.

Another swarm of anxious guests descended upon the front desk and Dani had to stand firm to maintain her position in line. She didn't feel quite so odd to be standing in only her stockinged feet. There was quite a wild assortment of strangely dressed people surrounding her, everything from a worn chenille robe to a sequined gown or two. It was obvious that some people were having no better luck than she had getting a phone line or reaching a hotel department.

Moments before it was her turn, a tall, gray-haired gentleman sporting a green golf shirt stepped behind the desk to assist the flustered clerks. By the way the two women greeted him, she knew he was part of hotel management.

Perfect. She knew how to handle this situation. It was always best to go to the top. She'd refuse to take no for an answer. She'd pull out all the stops if she had to. By golly, she'd get her own room *and* a crib.

As the woman in front of her moved away from the desk, Dani patted her bedraggled ponytail and curved her lips in an engaging smile. Squaring her shoulders, she stepped forward. And out of the corner of her eye, she noticed the familiar blonde.

About a yard away, within earshot, Bentley Brewster was talking to her companion. The same man whom

Dani had seen her with earlier. Quickly, Dani averted her gaze. She tried to focus on the man behind the desk, the one waiting with strained patience.

"Can I help you?" he asked for the second time.

"Hi." The word came out a lame croak.

He leaned forward. "I'm sorry, ma'am, you'll have to speak up."

"Do you…"

She stopped, her voice sounding abnormally high. It was impossible that the entire lobby full of people could shut up at the same time. But that's the way it sounded to Dani. She cast a quick, cautious glance at Bentley. So far the woman was still too deep in heated conversation with her companion to pay any attention to her.

"Can I help you, ma'am?" The manager's voice rose an octave.

She cringed, then whispered, "Where's housekeeping?"

"No guests are allowed in the back of the house. Can I help you with something?"

"A crib?" Her voice was barely a squeak. Someone jostled her from behind.

"A crib," he repeated a tad too loud, then frowned. "What's your room number? I'll check into it and give you a call."

Without a second thought about her rudeness, she grabbed the pad of paper and pen from the man's hand, scribbled Jack's name and room number across the top, and with a sheepish smile, scrambled as far away from Bentley Brewster as she could get.

Only when she got near the gift shop did she slow down. After a quick peek over her shoulder, she stopped long enough to lust after the thick half-pound

European chocolate bars sitting on display near the door.

"Don't even think about it, missy. I'm having a hard enough time marrying you off."

Dani halted at the familiar voice behind her. She shook her head. It couldn't be. A nervous giggle tickled the inside of her chest. She must be a whole lot more stressed than she thought.

She turned around, starting to smile at herself. Her lips froze midway. "Mom?"

JACK HADN'T BEEN too terribly upset after he got the call from the front desk. Sure, it would have been more convenient to have a crib, but if they did, Dani would be more likely to leave Sam alone with him.

What did upset him, however, was the fact that he'd received the call nearly an hour ago and that she should have returned already. She'd said she was going down to housekeeping. She'd never mentioned going anywhere else, and he knew she didn't have any money. Although earlier he'd encouraged her to charge anything she wanted to his room. Maybe she was just having a cup of coffee in the restaurant. Or a drink at the bar.

Or maybe she had found someplace else to stay for the night.

She would have called, he told himself, as he stepped out of the shower. Having left the bathroom door open, he would have heard the phone. Besides, everyone else and their dog had already called.

First it was Rik to see how they all were doing. Then Bentley had returned his earlier call, and Jack had been relieved to discover that he had no explaining to do whatsoever. Bentley had sounded vaguely distracted, and didn't have a clue about Dani and the key or her relationship to Jack. So he had decided to leave well enough alone on that front.

Babs Brewster's call was the problem. She wanted him to have lunch or a drink with her and her husband Dan tomorrow. In his haste to get her off the phone, Jack had foolishly agreed to a drink tomorrow afternoon. He wondered what she would have said if he'd asked to bring Sam.

The thought of her appalled expression cracking that aristocratic facade cheered him immensely as he toweled himself dry. Stephanie would appreciate that visual. He'd have to remember to tell her.

After knotting the towel around his waist, he stepped into the room for a fresh change of clothes and heard the door click open.

AFTER ALTERNATELY trying to get away from her mother and patiently listening to the woman rattle on for nearly an hour, Dani was still no closer to figuring out how the heck Mona had gotten here. She lived clear on the other side of the island and had absolutely no business at the Paradise Bay Hotel—except to make her only daughter's life miserable.

"I still don't understand why you'd come out in this weather, or how you managed to get here," Dani said, and instantly realized what a fool she was for bringing up the subject again. She knew damn well her mother could talk nonstop for a week and still not come to a reasonable point.

Mona's sigh was dramatic as she followed her out of the elevator and down the corridor toward Jack's room. "Okay, I'll be totally honest with you. You won't like it, mind you, but I'll give it to you straight."

Even though she knew better, even though she'd probably kick herself later, Dani slowed down and looked expectantly at her mother.

"There's a wedding in your future, very near future, in fact," Mona said, pausing for effect, and Dani mentally kicked herself. "But according to the alignment of stars, there is great possibility of disaster. I'm here to counteract that."

"Great." Dani kept walking. *Oh, yeah, there was going to be a wedding all right.* "Where did you get that sound piece of advice? From one of those free psychic readings?"

"Absolutely not." Mona added a little hop to her step in order to keep up. "I paid twenty bucks for it."

"Oh." Dani rolled her eyes as she inserted the key card into the lock. "Then it must be true."

As soon as the lock clicked open, it occurred to her that she shouldn't barge in on Jack with her mother in tow. Although she couldn't imagine what he'd be doing that could be inappropriate, knowing that she'd be returning.

She also considered that it probably wasn't such a hot idea for Mona to know that Dani had her own key to Jack's room. The fact that he was about to be married to someone else might be too minute a detail for her ever-imaginative mother.

But it was already too late, Dani realized, when she slid a peek at Mona who, with arched red eyebrows, looked on with far too much interest.

Sighing, Dani offered a token, warning knock before pushing the door open.

"There you are." Jack's smile faded as his gaze left her face and wandered over her shoulder to Mona.

Dani's gaze split from his in the same instant to settle at a point much lower. "Why are you only wearing *that?*"

Jack gave the knot at his waist a reassuring pat. The white towel wrapped snugly around his hips did nothing to hide the fact that he'd just had a rather exciting shower—or something.

"I wasn't expecting company," he said tightly. His hair was wet and looked nearly black, and he still hadn't shaved. Drops of moisture glistened off his tanned chest and nicely muscled shoulders.

He looked terrific.

Dani swallowed, closed her eyes and made a small deal with her Creator.

When she felt the nudge at her ribs, her eyes popped open and she slowly, hesitantly centered them on her mother.

"He's the one," Mona said calmly.

Dani stared at her with a growing sense of dread. The same tingling excitement she'd felt earlier in the crowded lobby swarmed her nerve endings. Mona was the high-strung, gabby type. She *never* sounded poised or nonchalant about anything. It was downright spooky to hear the confidence in her voice, to see the serenity in her overly made-up face.

"Dani?"

She dragged her gaze away from her mother. The way Jack was subtly scowling at her, she knew that this wasn't the first time he'd tried to get her attention.

"Yes," she snapped.

His scowl deepened. "Will you watch Sam while I go change?"

"Of course. I'll save the introductions," she said stiffly.

He gave her a dark look before grabbing a shirt and jeans and disappearing behind the bathroom door.

Dani crossed the room toward Sam knowing she had to look at her mother at some point, but wishing it didn't have to be in this decade.

"Why didn't you tell me?" Mona rushed over, her purple satiny caftan billowing around her slim body and clashing horribly with her bright red hair. And Dani felt a perverse comfort in the familiar wild gleam in her mother's green eyes, in the excitable way she tugged at Dani's arm.

"About Sam? I did."

"Not him." Mona stopped to ogle the baby. She peered in close and Sam giggled. "Oh, he is a cutie, though." Turning back to her daughter, her eyes narrowed. "Jack is perfect."

"Jack is getting married."

She smiled, batting her thick false lashes. "He certainly is."

"No, Mother. I mean he already *is* getting married. Haven't you listened to a word I've said?" Dani shook her head and addressed Sam, "Of course she hasn't. Why do I bother? Why did I think for one blessed minute that she could bail me out?"

Sam stopped laughing and kicking, and suddenly looking very solemn, he switched his wide-eyed gaze from Dani to Mona.

"I think fuchsia would be a good wedding color in this case," Mona said, squinting thoughtfully off into space. "With Jack's dark hair... Oh, and did you see that scrumptious patch of fur on his chest? My third husband had—"

"Mother, I will not hesitate to throw you out in this

storm.'' Dani's voice lowered in warning as her gaze darted to the bathroom door.

She should never have brought her mother here. Mona wasn't mean or malicious, but she had a one-track mind, especially when it came to her daughter. And something small and petty like an engagement between two childhood sweethearts, who'd probably been pining for each other for years, obviously wasn't going to deter her.

"Jack will be out at any minute," Dani said, then enunciating each word clearly and deliberately, she prompted, "Now, what are you going to ask him?"

Mona frowned in concentration. "If he likes fuchsia?"

She took a deep, cleansing breath. And to think she'd felt a moment's guilt for trying to give her mother the slip earlier. "You are going to ask him if you can help with the baby. You're going to tell him—"

Jack opened the door. As soon as he stepped into the room, the lights flickered. He glanced at the closed drapes. "It's done that twice tonight," he said.

"There's a good reason for this storm," Mona said, and that calm air about her was back, making every last hair on Dani's neck spring for the ceiling.

"Jack, this is my mother, Mona Crabtree," Dani said.

"It's Mona Humperdink." Her mother extended a youthful-looking hand. "Crabtree was my fourth husband's name. Just because Hump and I were only married a week doesn't mean the name isn't legal." Her frown dissolved into a smile. "And you're Jack."

Mona's gaze was blatantly assessing, starting from the bemused curve of his mouth, down to his flat stomach, and ending somewhere around his denim-covered thighs.

Dani forced a smile. "Will you excuse us for a minute?"

Mona shifted away when Dani would have grabbed her arm, and asked, "Tell me, Jack, what do you do for a living?"

Jack chuckled when he heard Dani growl. He watched the silent interchange between mother and daughter and his confusion quickly gave way to amused interest.

If someone had placed the two women in a lineup and made him choose, he would never have linked them in any way. Whereas Dani was of medium height, her mother wasn't a centimeter over five feet. And while Dani's hair was as dark as midnight, her mother's was a flaming red.

He squinted a little. The color had to be natural. No one in their right mind would choose that shade from a bottle.

"Why don't you have a seat, Mona?" he asked, smiling from her to Dani, who was giving him a don't-encourage-her look. He ignored it. "May I call you that?"

"Of course, especially since we'll soon be—"

"Mother was just leaving." From behind, Dani placed both hands on her mom's shoulders and urged her to the door.

"You can't change fate, Daniella," Mona said over her shoulder. Her dress was made of a crisp, shiny-looking fabric that made a swishing sound as she struggled to keep up with her daughter's pace.

"Wait a minute, Dani. Is your mother—" Jack headed them off. "Mona, where are you staying?"

"Well, I met this very hunky guy, who—"

"Mother." Dani put up a hand, cutting her off, then she glanced at Jack. "Don't ask her any questions. Trust me on this."

Mona shrugged. "I really do have to be going now. I have a date, and with the third moon hovering over Venus—"

"Call me later, Mother." Dani shouldered Jack to the side.

"You know where I'll be," Mona said, and Dani answered, "Yes, Mother" before she gently but firmly forced her mother out the door.

When the lock clicked into place, he said, "I don't believe it. You just threw out your own mother."

Her relief was tangible. "You can thank me later," she said as she ran an agitated hand through her hair. Her thumb snagged the elastic band holding her ponytail together and a heavy swath of hair tumbled free.

The black satin fell across her face onto her shoulder and rested on the top of her breast. And Jack was suddenly very glad that she *had* thrown her mother out. He didn't want to thank her later, either. He wanted to thank her now. Only he didn't think she'd appreciate what he had in mind.

"There is no crib," he said, curbing the many questions he had about her mother.

"They called?" She stopped pacing to look at him. When he nodded, she said, "Great. Now what?"

"We could sleep on either side of him."

Her hand flew through her hair again and the rest of the ponytail bit the dust. Other than that, she accepted his suggestion pretty well. At least she didn't deck him. She merely nibbled at her lower lip, her dark brows drawn together in thought. Then her eyes lit up. "How deep is your suitcase?"

His mouth twisted wryly. "I have a garment bag and a duffel bag."

She resumed her pacing. A minute later she stopped in front of the dresser. "I wonder if those drawers pull all the way out."

She was resourceful, he'd hand her that. Not because he was keen on the idea, but because he had to at least put in a show of support, he tried jimmying the drawer off the track.

"It's not budging," he said, and was proud of himself for keeping the smile out of his voice. "I guess we'll have to go with my idea."

He straightened and faced her. She was in clear need of convincing. The word *but* was already forming on her thinly stretched lips.

He shrugged. "Unless you want to ask your mother. Maybe she could sleep on one side of Sam." He relaxed his shoulders and, trying to look as pitiful as possible, let them sag a subtle inch. "I don't mind the hard floor."

She let her head drop back on her neck and scrubbed at her eyes. After staring at the ceiling for nearly a minute, she said wearily, "Okay."

His heart sped up. "Okay, we sandwich Sam? Or okay you'll get your mother?"

Slowly she let her chin drop forward and she slanted him a blank look. "Okay, I'll sleep with you."

Chapter Nine

Dani thought Jack was going to choke and she'd have to perform the Heimlich maneuver, something at which she was incredibly rusty.

She sighed, deciding that her deliberate play on words and the look on his face was all the fun she could handle for one night. "Relax, big guy, I didn't mean it like it sounded."

He exhaled loudly, his color returning to normal. "Hell, Dani, I didn't know you had this mean streak in you."

"Mona brings out the best in me."

"What is she doing here, anyway?" He loosened the neckline of his stretched-out T-shirt, and Dani bit back a grin.

"Who knows? In case you haven't noticed, she only plays with half a deck."

His eyebrows lifted as he slid her an admonishing look. "And you chastised me for ragging on Babs Brewster."

She grinned, feeling a trace of heat sting her cheeks. "You're right. Except I'd pit Mona against Babs any time. She'd win hands down for screwy mother of the year."

Sam started fussing and Dani scooted over to the bed and picked him up. "We're ignoring you, aren't we, sweetie? I'm so sorry." She wiggled a finger under his arm until he giggled. "I'm so sorry," she repeated in a singsong voice. "Yes, I am."

She kept playing with Sam, ducking as he tried to pull her hair, until she felt the weight of Jack's stare. Feeling a little self-conscious because she'd momentarily forgotten that he was there, she glanced at him.

His quizzical frown turned into a smile. "Why don't you have kids?"

"Are you crazy? They'd have Mona for a grandmother."

"I'm serious."

Me, too, was on the tip of her tongue but she could tell by his expression that she wouldn't get away with a flip answer. It hadn't escaped her notice that as soon as she'd picked Sam up, Jack had eagerly begun tugging down the quilt and preparing for bed. And she thought about stalling by making a crack about that, but she glumly realized she deserved this. She was the one who wanted to talk.

"I don't know." She shrugged, deciding to tiptoe down honesty lane. "I was busy with my career. Besides, I just turned thirty-one last month. I'm not over the hill yet."

He laughed, and she wasn't sure what he found so funny.

"Did you think I was older?" She squinted accusingly at him until she remembered that squinting emphasized crow's-feet, and she blinked.

"Younger."

"Good answer."

"I'm no dummy."

"Why did you laugh?"

"I guess I don't think of delivering babies in stork costumes as a career." A grin lurked behind his straight expression as he went back to turning down the bed.

She opened her mouth to correct his mistaken assumption, but quickly closed it. She didn't need anyone else telling her what a fool she'd been to give up the last ten years of her life. Which wasn't entirely accurate, anyway. She hadn't given up everything she'd worked for. She'd simply gotten tired of letting life pass her by, and had started a new chapter.

"It's Big Bird," she said instead. "Not a stork."

"My mistake." This time the grin blossomed. "So you haven't told me what this audition in Honolulu is for."

"Well, it's a little hard to explain—sort of a traveling musical troupe."

"And you want to...sing?"

Dani paused. She didn't think she could answer without bursting out laughing. The distraught look on his face was priceless. "No," she said finally, cutting loose with a smile. "I do know my limitations. I dance."

His gaze drifted down to her legs. "I'm not surprised. I mean, you sort of look like a dancer." Without apology, he continued his frank appraisal before gradually meeting her eyes. "What kind of dancing?"

"At some point, I studied them all—ballet, jazz..." She shrugged. "I even belly dance."

"Yeah?"

"Gee, I've never had that kind of reaction from a man before." Shaking her head at the lecherous yet comical lift of his eyebrow, she threw a pillow at him.

Still holding Sam, she used her free hand to help fold back her side of the comforter.

Dodging the pillow, he laughed. "Maybe you ought to practice, huh? Before your audition."

"No, thanks. I've had over twenty years of practice."

He let out a low whistle. "Talk about dedication."

"Not really. The alternative was going home to Mona and her husband du jour," she said, half joking. Although her mother's revolving-door marriages had been a problem when Dani was a child, she held no grudges as an adult.

"You really don't like her."

She laid Sam down, and looked up in surprise. "That's not true. I love Mona." She put up a hand to stall his budding interruption. "I even like her. I don't always like the things she says or does, but she's got a good heart and I know I can always count on her."

Although he said nothing, Jack frowned as though he didn't believe her.

And even though she knew she didn't have to defend herself or Mona, she said, "That's why I brought her up here. If we need help with Sam, she'll be here for us."

"I thought maybe you wanted a chaperone."

He was right. But she wouldn't admit it. "Do I need one?"

Clearly surprised by the turnaround, his smug grin ended up a lopsided smile. Holding up both palms, he said, "I'm harmless."

It was her turn to give him a frank appraisal and she did so with deliberate slowness, starting with his broad chest, each taut muscle molded by the soft green cotton of his T-shirt. "Are you?"

"Not if you keep looking at me like that."

Her gaze flew to his. So much for payback. His eyes had darkened to the color of rich, expensive chocolate and his nostrils flared slightly. A tic in his jaw reinforced the restraint for which he clearly battled.

"Tell me about Stephanie," she said quickly.

A knowing smile tugged at one side of his mouth. Then he moved his neck in semicircles as though he were trying to stretch out the tension. "I've told you everything."

Dani had some tension she'd like to get rid of herself, she decided as she watched the bunching and relaxing of his chest muscles. The room had heated up by ten degrees in the last few minutes, and for a crazy moment she didn't want to hear about Stephanie after all.

She wanted to watch Jack stretch and flex and...

"I think Sam is wet." Jack angled his head to get a better look at the baby. "How long do you think those rubber pants will hold out?"

"I guess if we keep rinsing them out we'll be okay."

"Maybe we ought to air dry it this time, huh?"

"I don't know. Letting him fly solo might be too risky. Don't forget, he's going to be sleeping between—" She bit off the last word when she saw what that reminder did to Jack's already dark eyes.

"Okay." He paced a few steps. "I've got an idea."

She watched him go to the closet as she stretched out the towel she used as a pad on which to change Sam. Then she pulled out one of the new T-shirts. They still had three disposable diapers left, but she hoped that figuring out this new diaper system would help take her mind off Jack.

He returned from the closet and held up a black and white plastic laundry bag. "This should work."

"How?"

"We'll lay the diaper on top and then put the whole thing on him at once."

"I don't know." She frowned at the rubber pants she'd just pulled off Sam. "I think these have elastic around the legs for a reason."

He thoughtfully regarded the strange article of baby clothing. "Maybe we could tie an extra strip around each of his legs."

"We'll cut off his circulation."

"Not tight."

"Then it won't work."

He scowled openly at her. "Why are you being so argumentative all of a sudden?"

"I'm not," she snapped, even as she realized that she was. Her tone was uncharacteristically snippy, and her nerves felt like they were being strummed with a wire comb. "I'm just trying to be realistic."

That was partially true. She was pragmatic enough to realize that sharing a room with him tonight might be asking for more trouble than she was up to handling.

As if to confirm her conclusion, her gaze was drawn to the nicely rounded bicep lifting the edge of his shirt-sleeve as he held up the plastic bag for further inspection, and her breath got all tangled up in her chest.

She quickly forced her eyes toward the bag and helplessly zeroed in on his large, well-kept hands. The brief fantasy of how they'd feel on her naked breasts gave her a hot flash. What in heaven's name was wrong with her?

When her attention finally made it to his face, she swallowed. Blatant desire smoldered in his eyes.

"You have a better idea?" He grabbed the hem of his shirt and yanked it up over his head.

"What are you doing?" She scooped up Sam as if he could protect her. And remembered too late that he was still wet and that she'd already removed his rubber pants.

"It's hotter than hell in here."

"Turn up the air conditioner."

"I already did."

"Then take a cold shower."

"That's next."

She didn't have anything to say to that. "Here." She passed Sam to him, feeling only a fleeting surge of guilt over the soggy diaper. "We need safety pins. You forgot safety pins." She made it to the door. "For his T-shirts. I mean, diapers. I'll have to get them."

"Dani, wait."

Her hand was already turning the knob and she knew he had nothing to say that she wanted to hear. There was absolutely no reason to stop, and every reason in the world to keep on walking. *Damn.* Calling herself the worst kind of idiot, she hesitated, but kept her back to him.

"Yes?"

"I have to ask you something."

She took a deep breath.

"If it weren't for Stephanie—"

She couldn't let him finish. Her hand moved and she heard the lock click its release. "I guess we'll never know," she said, and quickly slipped out the door.

DANI STOOD AT THE EDGE of the corridor where the wall barely met the canvas partition. She'd been to this hotel only once before but she vividly remembered that one of the things she liked most about the architectural design of the three buildings was the breezy, open-air feel to it. From any guest room floor, you had an unobstructed view of the ocean from one end of the corridor and a spectacular view of the mountains from the other.

Usually, there were no windows or screens or anything else to prevent the flow of the cool trade winds coming off the Pacific. The breeze was free to sail down the halls, and to bring with it the sweet fragrance of wild tropical flowers. Tonight, plain graying canvas sealed off the view, and thankfully, the gusting wind.

Gingerly she pried the canvas away from the wall. Even leaving just a narrow opening, the wind whipped through and stung her face. She jerked her hand away. She'd only wanted a little air, enough to cool her flushed cheeks.

Jack was getting to her. And she was allowing him to do so. Sighing, she edged back.

Even though she knew that the wind was too strong to be fooled with, she'd stepped up, brushed caution aside and asked for trouble. It was like putting your hand to the fire despite knowing you'd get burned. And she was doing the same thing with Jack.

She had no business spending the night in his room, even if that decision meant that she slept out here in the corridor. So why did she have this overwhelming urge to tempt fate? She could rationalize what she was doing in at least a half a dozen ways. Sam needed her, she wanted the privacy of a room, the comfort of a bathroom, a shower, and she did feel somewhat responsible for Jack's plight with Sam. It had been reckless of her to accept custody of the child in the first place.

So why hadn't she asked Mona for help as she'd

planned on doing? Jack was right. They did need a chaperone, and Sam deserved the care Mona could give him.

But Dani was already feeling out of kilter and there was no one on this earth that could keep her that way longer than her mother. And that final excuse would have to do, she realized as she set out to find the safety pins, because she just couldn't seem to make herself walk away from Jack.

THE WIND HADN'T let up since midafternoon. Jack almost dreaded the first light of morning when the inevitable destruction would be so clearly visible. The last he heard on the television was that the gusts had reached nearly seventy miles an hour. If they picked up any more speed, the local meteorologist would have to finally admit that this was more than a tropical storm.

He let go of the drapes, letting them fall into place. It was as black as sin out. He couldn't see anything anyway. Besides, only moments ago, someone on the hotel staff had slipped a general letter to all guests under the door, advising everyone to keep away from the windows. As an added precaution, they also indicated that they would be leaving candles outside the rooms later, in the event power was lost.

He wished Dani would hurry back, so that he could be sure she was safe.

Weather never bothered him much. Not even this kind. He'd seen all types of storms and floods and freak turns of nature down in South America. Hell, he'd had a lot less than bricks and drywall between him and a raging storm before, and easily lived through the experience. Rik had often accused him of getting a rush from living on the edge. And he guessed his friend's charge was fairly accurate.

But right now, his gut clenched and quivered as if he were a damn twelve-year-old getting ready for his first boy-girl party. Only it wasn't anything as fun and festive as a party that had him wound tighter than his favorite fishing rod reel. It was the ridiculous fact that he didn't know where Dani was or when she'd return.

And to top it all off, he was beginning to feel like a damn old hen, and that feeling stank, too.

Briefly closing his eyes, he tried to scrub the worry away. But an old experience pricked his memory instead, and he fleetingly relived the gut-twisting anxiety of waiting in the locker room as a rookie player, excited over his first professional game.

The next and last time Jack'd had that feeling, he'd been sitting across Dr. Wong's shiny cherry desk, listening to why he could never play football again.

He rarely thought about the past, and he was surprised to find himself thinking about it now. Maybe the flashbacks had to do with Stephanie and how she'd suddenly popped back into his life. She'd always been a significant part of his past, too. Now, she was going to be a part of his future.

For whatever reason, that thought held less appeal today than it had yesterday. Which wasn't saying much.

He liked Stephanie. He figured he even loved her in an abstract way. She'd been a good friend, the sister he never had. But thinking of her as his wife was going to be tougher than he'd thought.

Even now, he didn't feel the slightest trace of guilt for not worrying about her. He had no doubt that she was warm and safe, and sipping champagne, nibbling caviar, and laughing over her mother's hysterics because of the postponed wedding.

But that's all it was—a postponement, a short respite. Because in the end, there would be a wedding. Stephanie still needed a husband, and Jack would never go back on his word.

"Jack?"

Dani's voice behind him jerked him back to earth. He hadn't even heard her come in.

"I'm sorry I startled you," she said. "I did knock before I walked in."

"You don't have to do that." He put his hand out to her, and she stared at it with a perplexed look on her face. He couldn't help her out with an explanation, though. He wasn't sure why he'd done it or what he expected. "I'm glad you're back. I don't like you wandering around with all this high wind."

Her gaze lifted from his hand to his face, and she smiled. "I didn't go outside." Then she dropped three safety pins onto his palm.

He fisted the pins. "Sam's asleep again. I used one of the disposable diapers on him so we wouldn't have to wait." She nodded, and after a pause, he added, "I wish we could go down to the bar or something."

"You can go. There's no reason for both of us to be here." She pulled the elastic band from her hair and combed her fingers through. When he was too busy being mesmerized by the shiny blue-black strands that sifted through her fingers, she said, "Really. I don't mind staying at all. I'm sort of wiped out."

"No. I'm fine staying here. I just wish I could take you out for a while."

She shook her head. "Very bad idea. Stephanie's family has to be all over the place."

"Yeah, I'm sure Babs is running the hotel by now."

"Only if she can out talk Mona."

They both laughed, then he asked, "Did you notice if the band is playing in the bar?"

"It was so noisy in the lobby I couldn't tell you. Go ahead, Jack, give Rik a call. I truly don't mind staying."

"Nah." He grinned. "Rik makes a lousy dance partner."

She gaped at him. "You want to go dancing? Your bride is stranded on another island and you want to go pick up stray women to dance with?"

"Nope. I want to dance with you."

Her laugh was brief, humorless. "You're as bad as Mona. You don't listen to me, either."

"We can go down separately. Then I can slyly pick you up at the bar." He waggled his brows up and down.

She rolled her eyes. "That should make all the Brewsters really happy."

"No one will know. Besides, it's almost midnight, and they're all on California or Boston time. I'd bet they're all safely tucked away in their beds."

"It's still a bad idea."

"It's not. Call Mona. Ask her to watch Sam."

Dani worried her lower lip as she seemed to do when she was thinking hard on something. Although he'd never admit it to her, she was right. This was a crappy idea, and he wasn't sure what had come over him to suggest it. He didn't even like to dance. Hell, it had been so long since he'd tried hoofing it around a dance floor, he wasn't sure if he could remember how.

Except that as soon as she'd dropped the pins into

his hand he knew what he wanted. He wanted to feel her in his arms, to hold her and not have her pull away.

"Well..." It looked as though she might give in, then she briskly shook her head. "I'm not sure I could find Mona, or her, uh, friend. She's probably out partying herself. Anyway, I don't have anything to wear."

"Come on, we couldn't lose Mona if we tried." He grinned at her surprised look, watched it slide into outrage, then settle on a smirk. As her arms started to cross and her foot began to tap, he reached into a dresser drawer. "And...you have this."

She blinked at the white dress he held out to her.

Hugely pleased with himself, he patiently waited for her smile.

Her expression cooled. "Is that Stephanie's dress?"

"No." He frowned at her, then at the garment. "I bought it in the hotel boutique when I got the T-shirts."

He shook it out until the full skirt nearly touched the floor. There were two thin elastic bands at the top and the sales clerk said that the cuffed neckline could be worn on or off the shoulder. He'd only planned on telling Dani about the off-the-shoulder part. Now, he didn't think he should open his mouth at all.

She still didn't look too happy, but she tentatively put out a hand and touched the silky fabric.

"That was very thoughtful of you," she said, and drew back her hand to clasp with the other. No hint of a smile softened her lips.

"But?"

She turned away. "I don't think it's suitable."

"Suitable?" His hand fell to his side and the white silk puddled on the floor. "For dancing?"

She didn't answer. Instead, she descended into a

stubborn silence, and slanting him a sideways glance, started to fold the T-shirts he'd bought for diapers.

He jammed the dress back into the drawer and slammed it shut. From his peripheral vision, he saw Sam stir. He instantly felt bad for causing the racket but that didn't cool his temper any. Nor did telling himself that it shouldn't matter that she disliked the dress.

The wind chose that moment to wail through the cracks and Jack figured that that was plenty of justification for his foul mood.

Walking up to her, he pulled a T-shirt out of her hand. "Here you are a professional dancer, and I was willing to get out on the dance floor with you and make an ass of myself, and now I get the silent treatment because you don't like the dress?"

Shaking back her hair, her eyes met his. Bright and green, they sparkled with surprise. "I love the dress, Jack. It's beautiful."

His steam and shoulders both slipped a notch. "You said it wasn't suitable."

"It's not," she insisted, the light in her eyes dimming. "It looks like a wedding dress." She turned away. "And I'm not the bride."

Chapter Ten

It was almost one-thirty by the time Dani slipped between the cool white sheets and carefully settled in next to Sam. He had only been up once since Jack had gone to the bar, and she meant to keep it that way.

Although why she wanted all this downtime to think, she couldn't figure out. She didn't understand Jack, and she certainly didn't understand why she wanted another woman's man. This was so totally out of character for her, she honestly didn't know what to think or do.

However, she did know that a good night's rest was part of the answer. She was tired. Bone-crushingly tired. And with a little sleep, she was sure to have a better perspective on what was happening to her.

If she could just stop replaying old tapes in her head.

It was a difficult task, though, to get the picture of Jack's hurt face out of her mind. He'd thought that she didn't like the dress, that she hadn't appreciated his considerate gesture. But that hadn't been the problem at all. It was the reminder that stung.

The reminder that Dani was flirting with the role of the Other Woman.

Although she couldn't prove the allegation, nor did she have any desire to do so, Dani was fairly certain

Mona had received star billing in that particular role a couple of times. It wasn't that her mother was callous or spiteful, but she'd always placed far too much weight on the alignment of stars and the preponderance of fate and not quite enough on another person's previous claim.

And as much as she loved her mother, Dani often disapproved of the means to Mona's ends.

She switched from lying on her side to her back and watched a sliver of a shadow promenade across the ceiling. And in spite of herself, she wondered who Jack was dancing with now. He'd been gone for nearly an hour. Plenty of time to have picked up three women if he chose.

As if summoned by her thoughts, the door clicked and Jack crept in. The bathroom light shone through where she'd left the door partially open, and before she could close her eyes and pretend she was asleep, he looked at her and winked.

She didn't acknowledge him, but watched him steal soundlessly across the room, and wondered if he was drunk.

He hadn't left angry exactly, but he hadn't been in a good enough mood to come back winking, either. She supposed she should be a little afraid if he was drunk, since she really didn't know this man, but then again, this was Jack. And, although it went against reason, she possessed not an ounce of fear.

After rummaging through a dresser drawer, then disappearing into the bathroom for a few minutes, he returned to the room in a pair of skimpy red running shorts. He turned the bathroom light off before slipping into his side of the bed, and Dani sort of wished he'd left it on.

Her side of the mattress plumped up as he settled in, and she felt a rush of heat with the tangible proof that they were in the same bed. Instantly, she decided that they were better off without the light, after all.

At least a minute passed and Jack said not a word. He knew that she was awake and she wondered if he expected her to make the first move, to apologize maybe, or perhaps just to say good-night.

"Jack?"

"Dani?"

They both whispered at the same time, and she smiled with relief into the darkness.

"You go first," he whispered, and she could tell by his voice that he was smiling, too.

"I was just going to say—was the bar crowded?" Inane, she knew, grimacing at the dark ceiling. But she'd had a sudden attack of shyness and asked the first thing that popped into her head.

"I don't know. I didn't go there."

"Oh."

"I went for a walk."

"Outside?" Her voice had risen and she bit her lip, waiting with dread for Sam to fuss. He didn't turn a hair.

"Hardly. I just sort of roamed the corridors and banquet levels."

"Oh."

No one spoke for another minute, until the howling wind pilfered the tentative silence.

"Dani?"

"Jack?"

They both laughed softly after they again spoke at once.

"You first this time," Dani whispered.

Another brief silence, then he said, "I'm sorry about the dress."

"Me, too. I mean, I'm sorry I gave you a hard time."

"No. I'm trying to say that I understand why you were upset. I didn't at first, but I do now."

"It was silly, really."

"No, it wasn't. I honestly understand."

The mattress dipped slightly toward his side, and she knew that he'd shifted. But the room was pitch-black and she couldn't tell where that movement placed him. Then she felt motion above her head near the rattan headboard, the stroke of a hand maybe. Or then again, she may have imagined it.

"Okay," she said. "We both already know this entire situation is awkward."

He chuckled, the sound low and raspy, and she took a deep breath before continuing. "So I propose that we agree to—" She stopped. Something fluttered just above her head and she swatted at it. "Are there bugs in here?"

"Hmm? I didn't see any."

Great. Now she was chasing shadows. "Okay, the way I see it—" This time she didn't see anything, but she felt the top of her hair stir. She raised her head off the pillow and squinted into the darkness. "Jack, I think we've got mosquitoes in here. Big ones."

"They wouldn't be out in this wind. Trust me."

"They have to go somewhere. Maybe you let some slip by when you came in?"

"Not a one. I promise."

"Okay." She let her head drop back onto the pillow. "Then where was I?"

"You were saying the hell with all this formali—"

"I don't think so. You're not paying attention again."

"Oh, yes, I am." A smile echoed in his voice.

"I just think we need to be adult about this."

"I couldn't agree more."

"Fine."

"So, let's do some adult things."

"Jack." She tried to make the single word warning sound stern, but whispering made that hard to do.

"I meant talk, Dani." His tone was all innocence now, but he'd drawled his previous words in a low and sexy voice, and she knew he was purposely messing with her.

"Really? I was hoping—" She cut herself off with a wistful, throaty sigh.

His side of the mattress really dipped this time and she had to cover her mouth to keep from laughing aloud. The instant she composed herself, she finished with, "I was hoping that you'd grown up in the last hour."

He laughed. "I *am* all grown-up. I've got the right parts and everything. Wanna see?"

"Why does everything end up being about sex with you?"

"Because you turn me on."

"Oh."

This time her side of the bed sagged as she shifted uneasily. She stared at the ceiling, her eyes wide, her blood zinging through her veins at an alarming rate, and she wondered what happened to that bone-crushing weariness she'd felt only minutes ago.

"Dani? I think there's something you should know about me." He paused, allowing a disturbingly long silence to elapse, making her think maybe he was reconsidering what he'd been about to say.

She didn't try to coax him. She simply stared into the darkness, not sure if she wanted any more information on Jack Keaton. What she already knew, she liked far too much.

He cleared his throat. "About Stephanie, and this, uh, marriage—"

"Wait, Jack."

"Another bug?"

"No. I want you to think about what you're going to say."

"What?" His tone carried a touch of irritation, or maybe he was just puzzled.

"You don't sound sure," she said gently. "I don't want you to say something you'll regret later."

Silence swelled and twisted until he let out a short vicious curse that startled her. Although it was muttered under his breath, it wasn't language he normally used.

"I'm sorry, Jack. I was only trying to help."

"Ah, Dani, I know that. That's who you are. That's one of the things that makes you so special." When he paused, she felt something again stir above her head. The motion feathered her hair and sent a shiver of anticipation down her neck into her belly. No mosquito had done *that* before.

"And that's precisely why I've got to explain," he continued, sounding even more irritated now. "Do you understand?"

No. She didn't understand at all. She didn't even know if she should be flattered or made indignant by his remark. Sinking a little deeper into her pillow, she pulled the sheet up to her chin. Stopping him didn't qualify her for sainthood. She wasn't just trying to protect him. She needed to protect herself, as well. It was difficult enough to share his bed and not touch him, she didn't want him to say anything that would shatter her fragile defenses.

"I shouldn't have met you," he said. "Not today."

She laughed softly. "You shouldn't have met Sam, either. Mona would claim it was fate." Sam was a safe subject. So was Mona. If she thought about her mother, Dani wouldn't have to worry about her mind being lured to dangerous territory. Mona was a good reminder that there were certain roles in life that Dani didn't want to play.

"And what would she say it meant?" he asked softly.

She groaned at the possibilities. Okay, so she was wrong. Mona was a bad topic, after all. "Speaking of my mother, I already talked to her about helping you with Sam. She'll be happy to do it."

"Helping *me?*" He shifted, making the mattress jiggle a little, and although it was too dark for him to do so, she could tell he was trying to look at her. "Are you trying to tell me something?"

"I'm hoping to get a ride out of here tomorrow morning."

"The road will be repaired?"

"No. Her rescue worker friend may be able to help me get to Kahului, though."

"It won't do you any good. You won't make it to Honolulu."

Her head jerked up and she peered through the darkness at him. "Did they close the airport? Have you heard something?"

"I didn't have to. Don't forget that I make my living

flying choppers. No one is going to fly in this wind. I guarantee you that.''

"Yeah, well, I'd still rather be waiting at the airport.'' She dropped her head back onto the pillow and returned her gaze to the ceiling. "I don't know how they're going to handle the mass exodus of tourists off the island, but if it's by lottery I want to be the first in line.''

He didn't say anything for a long time and just when she thought he'd fallen asleep, he said, "Tell you what, if you can't get a quick flight out of here, I'll fly you over myself.''

"You? You can't do that.''

"Why not?''

"You don't have a plane or helicopter for one thing.''

"Rik does.''

"Here? I thought he was your partner.''

"He is—or was, I should say. He's starting his own aerial tour business between Maui and Oahu. He'll be moving to Honolulu within a month.''

Dani squinted in his direction, wishing she could see his face. His blank tone revealed nothing, and she couldn't tell whether this was good or bad news. "Where does that leave you?'' Before he could answer, realization struck. "Ah, Stephanie will take his place.''

"Steph? Living on the Amazon?'' He burst out laughing, and Sam made an angry noise. "Sorry, buddy,'' Jack whispered, and when he passed a soothing hand over the baby's head, his thumb brushed her cheek at the same time.

His hand froze, maintaining contact with her skin, and she sucked in a breath, wishing for things she couldn't have, then wishing she hadn't. When she slowly exhaled, his thumb continued the path to her jaw before his touch slipped away.

"Stephanie lives in Honolulu," he said.

"But after you're married..." Her voice trailed off as a sudden thought occurred to her, and her heart slammed against her breastbone. "You're moving to Honolulu?"

Although she hadn't meant for it to come out that way, her tone sounded accusing and she silently cursed the jumble of emotions that tore at her insides and tossed her off track. Jack Keaton living half a world away was one thing. Living in her backyard was quite another.

"No." His voice was tight and controlled, and for an instant, she hated him for his composure.

"I mean after you two—"

"That's what I wanted to talk to you about." His hand returned to her face, and unerringly his palm pressed against her heated cheek.

She turned her head until he was forced to withdraw his hand. She didn't want him to touch her, not only because he didn't have the right, but because she didn't have the right to be touched by him, either.

"Okay, that was wrong," he said, "because you don't understand the situation. And that's one of the things I admire about you. That's also the reason I've made a decision to admit something about Stephanie and me."

"I don't want to hear this." She pressed one ear into the pillow, the other she covered with the arm she threw across the side of her head.

His laugh was short, confused. "Why not?"

She closed her eyes and bit her lip. She knew what he was going to say, and she didn't want to hear it.

Dani wasn't as modern as he probably thought she was, and in spite of Mona, she certainly didn't approve of open marriages.

And she liked Jack. He was kind to Sam, he was concerned for her welfare, he was even willing to fly her to Honolulu. She probably liked him too much, in fact, but she didn't want him to fall from grace now.

"I think we should get some sleep," she whispered, curling up on her side and hugging her pillow. "Sam will be up soon and we'll both be wiped out."

"I just want to explain why I'm not moving to Honolulu," his said, his tone low and cautious.

"You're not?"

"No. Not much call for Amazon tour guides here."

"But if Stephanie isn't moving..." She stopped, and straightening, turned toward him. Her mind raced forward, tossing up ideas and discarding them with dizzying speed, until it braked on one. "So you need to find a job. Right?"

"Not exactly."

"Can't you continue your partnership with Rik?"

"No. I—"

"Okay, then what else have you done?"

"Dani?"

"Have you ever coached football?"

"Yeah, but—"

"Well, this is good. I could make a call tomorrow." One part of her brain reminded her that she didn't want him here, the other half was too damned relieved that she'd misconstrued his intentions. "I have some connections at the university—"

Jack started laughing. It was a deep, rumbling belly laugh, and even when Sam grumbled at the disturbance, Jack couldn't seem to stop. Although he obviously tried to contain himself, the bed shook with a fresh bout of silent laughter.

In spite of her annoyance on Sam's behalf, Dani couldn't help the contagious smile that tugged at her lips. "What?"

His amusement subsided to a soft chuckle, and he said, "I'm not looking for a job."

"But I thought—"

"I know. And you *kept* thinking and talking and thinking and talking. Hell, I wouldn't rag on Mona anymore if I were you."

"What's that supposed to mean?"

His effort to tamp down renewed laughter was obvious. "It means," he said, and she felt the stirring near her hair again, "that the apple doesn't fall far from the old tree."

She blinked, her breath caught, and to her horror, she felt the hot sting of tears prick her eyes. She blinked some more and quickly chased them away as she scooted down deeper into the covers and curled herself into a ball.

Her emotions had zigged and zagged all day. She was too tired to think, too tired to summon her sense of humor. She loved Mona. She even liked her most of the time. But she didn't want to be like her at all. No way, no how.

"Dani?"

She sniffed, then covered it with a cough.

"I was only joking."

"I know. Let's get some sleep, huh?"

"Something's wrong. Tell me."

"Nothing." She tried to put a smile in her voice. There was no need to tell him that he'd hit a sore spot, that he'd probably been closer to the truth than he knew. "I'm just tired."

"What I have to say won't take long. It's important." The urgency in his voice made her wary. It was clear that he'd come to a major decision, and she sensed once again that he was on the verge of saying something he might regret, something she might regret even more.

"Let's talk tomorrow, okay?" She glanced at him with new caution, this time grateful for the darkness, and a little saddened by the knowledge that it wasn't going to be hard to share a bed with him, after all.

Chapter Eleven

Half the sidewalk along the beach was gone. Large chunks of concrete had been lifted by the tide and sucked out to sea, leaving gaping pits where littered white sand met the hotel grass. A massive palm tree had been uprooted at the south end of the two-story hotel beach wing and lay fallen barely three feet from the building.

Jack's hand hovered near the drapery cord. He was tempted to close the curtains again. There wasn't any sunshine to let in anyway. No glorious dawn pinks and salmons like he'd seen the first two days after he'd arrived on Maui. But then again, the ugly black had disappeared, too. The sky was a palette of charcoal grays and the wind had died down a little since last night.

He didn't have much hope that the storm was over, though. The wind was still strong enough to do some major damage. Unless conditions changed drastically, Dani wasn't going to be flying anywhere today.

He heard the shower shut off and, deciding to leave the drapes open, he left his post at the window to check on Sam. He wanted to be sure that the baby was still dry and happy before Dani got out of the bathroom.

She'd done more than her share of caring for the child. Especially since they'd all awakened an hour ago.

In fact, she'd been so busy with Sam, she'd barely spared Jack a glance.

He picked Sam up and cradling him to his chest, he took the little guy to the lanai door for a look outside. The baby's eyes widened as he followed the movement of the coconut fronds, then he reached out both hands trying to grab the leaves as they thrashed the glass.

Laughing and kicking, Sam's compact little body showed an amazing amount of strength as he tried with all his might to catch the elusive fronds. Jack laughed, too, enjoying the temporary distraction from his troubled thoughts.

Something was bothering Dani. He understood part of the problem. In spite of the spark and sizzle between them, Jack was about to be married to someone else. She had no way of knowing that he wasn't entering into a true marriage, one that would never be consummated. And he admired her principled decision not to trespass.

Yet she'd also discouraged him from explaining. Although he hadn't tried too hard to overrule her either. Because explaining would make him a traitor. And he owed Stephanie more loyalty than that. He owed it to himself not to live with that kind of dishonor.

While he calmly, rationally told himself all this one minute, his confusion doubled in the next. Would Steph begrudge him this chance at happiness? What if Dani was the *one?* What if he'd been wrong when he told Rik that this hoax could work because he had no interest in marriage, in a family? After all, what did he have to offer anyone?

He was nothing but a has-been football hero who had forgotten how to live in civilization.

The bathroom door opened, and when he saw Dani standing there in his too large burgundy T-shirt, her eyes dull from weariness, his heart thudded and he figured he knew the answers to most of his questions.

Her hair was still wet from her shower and hung in black ropes around her face, making her look too pale. He saw her shoulders sag a fraction and he made a decision.

"Are you hungry?" he asked.

"Not particularly."

"Okay. Since Sam is all set, how about we skip breakfast and have an early lunch?"

"Fine." She walked to the dresser and fished out the brush he'd bought her. "If you don't need me for anything, I'm going to blow-dry my hair."

"No. You're going to take a nap."

"What?" She stopped halfway to the bathroom and laughed. "We just got up."

"No, we didn't. You've been up for hours."

Giving an annoyed toss of her head, she didn't refute him but instead looked pointedly at Sam, who was kicking and gurgling and seemed to have enough energy to run a marathon. "I think you forgot about our friend here."

"Nope. My little pal and I discussed it already and we're going for a walk."

"You can't traipse around the hotel with him."

"It's early yet. The Brewsters are all sound asleep."

"What happened to them being on mainland time?" She lifted one dark skeptical brow at the alarm clock. It read seven-thirty. "If you want to go out for a while, I can watch Sam."

"Sorry. This isn't open for discussion. Besides, we thought we'd go wake up Uncle Rik."

"Oh, he'll be happy about that."

"Tough. He's got to start proving himself as best man."

"Except the baby usually comes after the wedding."

"Very funny."

She grinned, and he immediately felt better. "Don't forget, he may have company."

"All the more reason to disturb him."

"Jack," she cautioned, but her lips were still slightly curved, making the room brighten like the sun had come out.

"As my best man it's his duty to be frustrated right along with me."

Her light mood promptly vanished and he was sorry he'd made the remark.

"Try to sleep for at least another hour, okay? Sam and I will go see if we can find that concierge." He switched the baby to his other arm and grabbed the pacifier out of the basket. "The kid's mother has got to be frantic by now, but I guess we can forget about her still being in the hotel."

She nodded. "I doubt I can sleep."

"Give it a try, okay?" Still cradling Sam with one arm, he reached for the drapery cords and drew the drapes until the room started darkening. "I'll bring back some news on the storm."

"Why are you trying to get rid of me?"

Smiling, he made it to the door but lingered there. "We thought it was the other way around."

"It's your room."

"It's going to be my funeral if I don't find Sam's

mother. I appreciate your helping out in the mean-time.''

"I don't need your gratitude." She stiffened, and he realized their conversation had taken a sudden, troublesome turn. "I feel a little responsible. I had no business delivering a baby."

"Know what? Everything will seem better once you've had some more sleep. And then we'll have our talk."

"I don't mean to sound querulous." She looked away. "I respect the way you've handled the situation. You've taken good care of Sam when you could have just washed your hands of him. And you've been aboveboard with me." She returned her gaze to meet his levelly. "When we say goodbye later I want to hold on to that respect. Do you understand?"

"Yeah. I understand," he said as he slipped out the door. And he did. He knew all about loyalty and respect. So why was she making it so damned hard for him to keep his promise to Stephanie?

"OH, NO. You're not going through with it," Jack said, having totally forgotten about the party. He ruffled the back of his head, dragged his hand down to his neck to work on the kinks forming there. With his other hand, he held Sam against his chest. "I don't even want a bachelor party."

"Sorry, pal. It's tradition." Rik clapped him on the shoulder, then tweaked Sam's chin. The baby laughed, then put both his arms out for Rik to take him.

Jack reared his head back in surprise. "I've never seen him do that before. You wanna try holding him?"

"Sure." His friend scooped up Sam by his armpits and swung him gently in the air a couple of times before bringing him to his chest. The baby batted happily at Rik's chin and he laughingly ducked out of the child's reach.

Jack gave him a funny look. "What the hell is this?" He slowly swung his gaze toward Rik's closed door, more interested than ever in the woman his friend was sharing his room with. And the reason why they had to stand out in the corridor. "Are you practicing for daddyhood or something?"

"You never know," Rik said, grinning, and Jack didn't miss the quick glance his friend tossed at the closed door. "Let's take a walk, huh?"

"I can't go too far. I don't want to run into any of the Brewsters."

"Let's head for the laundry room. We certainly won't find any of them there," Rik said dryly.

Exhaling loudly, Jack glared at his friend. He didn't want to hear one word of Stephanie-bashing today. He didn't want to hear about how rich and spoiled she was, and how he was a damned fool for going through with this wedding. He felt guilty enough.

One side of Rik's mouth lifted. "What's wrong with you? I hope your lack of sleep was a result of, uh, what was her name?"

"Can it."

Rik laughed at Jack's deadly look. "I guess not."

Sam started fussing and Jack slipped him the pacifier, then offered to take him from Rik.

He shook his head and frowned. "Did you give him breakfast?"

"Of course I did. Why?"

"What did you feed him?"

Jack laughed. "As if you would know the difference."

"I might."

Jack squinted at his friend. "What do you know about this baby?"

Rik gave him a yeah-right look. "You need some sleep, pal. Can't you get what's-her-name to watch him?"

"Her name is Dani." Jack knew he sounded testy as soon as he saw the sly, interested grin tug at his friend's mouth. He ignored him. "She's exhausted. I'm taking the kid for a walk so that she can sleep."

His friend frowned thoughtfully, then a twinkle lighted his eyes. "Tell you what. I'll keep him for a while and you can both get some rest."

Jack snorted. "Can't you be more obvious, Austin?"

Rik grinned and returned his attention to Sam.

They continued walking and Jack thought about how crazy life had gotten in the past couple of days. Even Rik was acting strangely. Although he'd made his opinion of Jack's decision perfectly clear, Rik was a traditional guy, and it wasn't like him to encourage Jack to cheat on his fiancée—especially since Rik didn't know the whole story.

Which reminded Jack to be suspicious of the bachelor party.

"About tonight," he said as they came to the end of the corridor and stopped to look out at the swelling waves clawing the beach. "We have to cancel the party."

"No way." Rik grunted his exasperation. "Everything's all set up."

"You're crazy. The staff is so overworked that they can barely handle room service. I doubt they'll object if we cancel."

"Forget it. You're not weaseling out of this party. I've been looking forward to it for too long."

Jack groaned, not liking the wicked and ominous timbre of Rik's voice. "I don't have anyone to baby-sit Sam."

"Ask Dani."

"Yeah, right. I can just hear me asking her to watch Sam while I go—" He stopped, briefly closed his eyes, then with pure dread, slid his friend a sideways look. "There aren't going to be any naked women at this *soirée*."

"Jack," Rik drawled out the name as if offended. Then his mouth curved mischievously. "Would I do something like that?"

Jack muttered a curse. Normally, he wouldn't think Rik would, but lately nothing surprised him.

"Look, either we'll have the party like we planned. Or I'll bring the party to you. Which is it?"

"You come to my room with *anyone* and you're dead meat."

Rik's grin broadened. "I take it you'll show up on time then?"

"Blackmail is an ugly business, Austin, and payback is hell."

Rik's smile faded, his brows drawing together. "I don't get it. You were all for this party three days ago."

"I was never all for it. I was willing to go along with it."

"Yeah, okay, maybe you weren't that enthusiastic, but you weren't being anal about it, either."

Jack massaged the base of his neck. "Things change."

Rik's frown deepened. "You wanna talk?"

"Nope. What time's the party?

"Eight."

"I'll be there, but if I'm late, no one comes to my room," Jack said. "Got it?"

"Yeah, I got it."

Jack reached for Sam, his mind already spinning, trying to come up with a story to tell Dani. He hated lying to her, but somehow he didn't think she'd appreciate having to change diapers while he was out partying...especially if the partying included women in any stage of undress.

And truthfully, he wasn't interested, either. He only had a couple of days of freedom left and he wanted to spend them with her.

"Are you okay?"

"What?" Jack looked at Rik and realized that although he'd been trying to take Sam from his friend, Rik had moved the baby out of range and Jack was standing with his arms out and empty. He blinked and spread his hands wider. "Yeah, fine. Give me the kid."

"I'm keeping Sam for a while."

"Nah. Dani will probably get ticked off if I come back without him."

Rik's eyebrows met in a dumbstruck expression. Slowly he looked at Sam, then back at Jack, a speculative gleam entering his eyes. "Too bad. Get some sleep. He'll be okay with me."

"I don't know..." Jack scrubbed at his eyes, his hair. His hand slid around to his jaw and he rubbed it, sighing wearily. He'd forgotten to shave again.

Laughing, Rik waved a hand in Jack's face, causing Jack to start. "How many fingers am I holding up?"

"How many am I?" Jack growled, his hand shooting up.

Rik laughed harder. "Hey, not in front of the kid. Get me some extra diapers and his bottle, then go hit the sack." He hesitated, that speculative gleam returning. "But if you're not in any hurry, maybe we should go see how much cholesterol we can swallow first?"

Jack shook his head. Breakfast was the last thing on his mind. "Some other time. I've got diapers to wash."

THE ROOM WAS STILL DARK. Outside, the wind still screeched its discontent. Dani barely kept one eye open. She lifted her head an inch and tried to focus on the digital clock, but quickly decided that it was too much trouble. She let her cheek sink back into the soft feather pillow as her eye drifted closed.

Although she usually tried to not to sleep on her stomach, she felt far too lethargic to flip over. Instead she hugged the pillow with her right arm, burrowing her face deeper into the downy softness. On her left, Sam cuddled close to her side.

Smiling lazily into the pillow, she moved her arm and gently rubbed his head. His hair felt coarse and crisp, and her brows drew sluggishly together. But she swiftly relaxed again, unwilling to relinquish this dreamy state, and her fingers lightly splayed the springy curls.

Yawning, stretching one leg out, she prodded herself to turn over, and pressed a drowsy kiss atop Sam's head.

Even in her sleepy state she knew something wasn't right. Forcing her eyes partially open, she frowned at how dark Sam's hair looked, how tanned his head was. She was so close, her lips only a breath away, that she had to squeeze back a smidgen in order to bring him into focus.

And Sam's head turned into Jack's chest right before her sleepy, disbelieving eyes. It was bare and furry and brushing her sensitive lips. She blinked, sputtered, tried to scoot away, but his arm swung over to wrap around her waist.

She tried to yell at him to release her but her brain and mouth wouldn't connect and a low guttural sound came out instead.

"Shhh, honey. Sleep," he mumbled without opening his eyes.

His words were barely intelligible, his breathing heavy, and her irritation ebbed as she realized he really was asleep. She was still annoyed, though, that he'd gotten in bed with her in the first place and she shoved at his arm.

But it was deadweight and wouldn't budge. When she started to turn over, he tightened his hold until her breasts were crushed against the side of his chest. Her entire body froze, and allowing only her eyes to move, her gaze darted to his face.

His lashes lay heavy on his cheeks and his lips parted ever so slightly. His jaw sported at least two days' worth of growth and obscured the grooves bracketing his mouth. Grooves that deepened attractively when he smiled.

She could tell by the rich, steady rhythm of his breathing that he wasn't faking sleep, and the temptation to watch him was enormous. Oh, she'd already memorized every detail of his face, like the tiny scar along his jawline and the devilish arch of his right eyebrow. But it was the private closeness that felt so alluring, forbidden. Which, of course, it was.

On a heartfelt sigh, she shoved at his arm until he shifted its weight, then scooted her body out from underneath it. He moaned, groping for her. His aim was impeccable and he cupped one breast. Dani took a deep breath, ready to flee the bed, and ended up filling his palm more fully. A heat wave swelled over her and she briefly closed her eyes.

When she opened them, she found that he'd chosen that moment to open his eyes, as well.

Slowly, he blinked once...twice. "Mornin'." A sleepy smile inched across his face. He flexed his palm. Her hardened nipple pressed its center.

Dani flew out of bed. Not until her feet hit the floor and she swung around to glare at him did he seem to notice where he was and what he'd been grabbing.

He looked at his empty palm, fisted it loosely, then released it, and looked up at her, his gaze skimming her chest and resting on her flushed face.

Her nipples were as hard as erasers and poking at the soft worn fabric of her borrowed T-shirt. Even worse, her heavy breathing was accentuating that humiliating fact. But she couldn't control the short rapid breaths any more than she could the pulse that nearly leaped through her wrists.

"What are you doing?" she sputtered.

"Not staying awake enough to enjoy it, whatever it is," he said, and the befuddled expression on his face knocked half the wind out of her sails.

A nervous laugh tickled her throat, but she swallowed it back and with a stern tone, she asked, "What were you doing in bed with me?"

He blinked again, and the confusion was replaced by wariness. "I'm sure you'll tell me."

"You know what I mean."

His gaze slid to her breasts, then quickly returned to

her face. He frowned, still looking puzzled. "Sleeping?"

"You were supposed to be taking Sam for a—" Her gaze flew around the room. "Where's Sam? What did you do with him?"

"Rik's got him."

"What's he doing with him?"

"Probably changing his diaper by now." Raking back his hair, Jack yawned. "Wish I could see that. What time is it, anyway?"

They both looked at the digital clock at the same time.

"Whoa. It's that late?" Jack sat up. The sheets bunched at his waist and Dani stepped back. One of his eyebrows hiked up as did the left side of his mouth. "I've got on shorts."

"I knew that." She tugged at the hem of her T-shirt. It nearly met the hem of her shorts—the same ones she'd worn yesterday.

Still smiling, he rubbed at his eyes, his jaw, down the front of his neck. Trying not to be obvious, she eyed the width of his chest, the thatch of dark hair that fanned out between his flat brown nipples and tapered at his narrow waist. His skin was deeply tanned but smooth and not leathery looking.

When she finally raised her gaze to his face, his brown eyes bored into hers and twinkled with amusement.

Oh, boy. She took a quick breath. "I hope you know it's not healthy to get that much sun." She cringed inwardly at the inane statement, then headed for the bathroom.

"Where are you going?"

"To get dressed." Which was another stupid remark. She was already dressed. She had no more clothes. But if she admitted that she needed a splash of icy water across her face, he'd misconstrue that remark for sure.

"Come back. Rik won't return Sam until I call for him."

That was supposed to entice her back to bed? Against her better judgment, she stopped and, turning halfway around, she said, "So?"

"So..." He patted the spot next to him.

His face was a solemn mask, the extra growth of beard giving him a roguish appeal, and if he thought for one second her returning to bed showed a lick of sense, he was either an idiot or...

Her expression clearly gave away her thoughts, because he grinned, and raising his hand from the area he'd been patting, he allowed his open palm to hover over the bed, slowly, farther and farther toward the opposite, safer edge.

His eyes never left hers as his grin broadened and he asked, "Am I getting warmer?"

Oh, yeah. She nearly choked on the thought, hyperventilated at the stunning picture he made. Eclipsing the short rattan headboard, his shoulders seemed even broader and more tanned, framed as they were by the snow-white walls. Well-developed muscles rounded nicely under his nipples and his stomach was taut and flat.

Straightening, she crossed her arms over her chest. "It's nearly one-thirty. And while you may have the desire to sleep the day away, I don't."

Jack laughed. Drawing back his hand, he raked it across his chest in a purely male gesture. "Who said anything about sleeping?"

Chapter Twelve

Watching her eyes widen first with disbelief, and then disgust, Jack knew he had to tell her. Today. Now. Before Rik brought Sam back—before the bachelor party. He smirked to himself. Before some other small disaster like the hurricane got in the way.

The situation was getting too complicated. This wasn't merely about loyalty to Stephanie anymore. She'd understand. She was a good friend. Her appeal for help had evolved out of desperation and at the time, he'd been willing to pick up the gauntlet. But right now, it seemed as though their deal had been forged in another lifetime. Only he had a lot of years left ticking in this one and he couldn't ignore this opportunity.

Jack didn't believe Stephanie would want him to, either. She'd want him to go for the magic.

He settled his attention on Dani who stood gaping at him. Even with her badly tousled hair, even with the sleep line that creased her left cheek, she looked beautiful. Almost as beautiful as her strength of character that kept her at arm's length from an engaged man.

He wanted to stay where he was and look at her all day. But his lower body was having an embarrassing reaction to the swell of her breasts against his old

T-shirt, and he was too far past seventeen to sit here and ignore the sign of trouble that problem could cause.

He didn't have to worry for long. After clearing her throat, she started to spout the wisecrack that undoubtedly hovered on the tip of her tongue.

Smothering a grin, he held up a hand. "Before you feed me to the sharks, I have something to tell you."

She stared hard for a long minute, uncertainty creasing her brows. "If it's an apology, I'm not interested." Then she spun about and resumed her trip to the bathroom.

"Dani…"

This time, she held up a hand and swung it out at an angle from her body, palm facing him, but didn't turn around or stop. "And if it's another suggestive remark or double entendre, I'm definitely not interested." She walked to the bathroom, and stood poised with her fingertips brushing the doorknob. "In fact, if it's even more than one syllable. I am *not* interested."

Without a backward glance, she slammed the door.

Jack squinted for a minute of confused silence, then a blade of anger sliced through him. What the hell was she so bent out of shape for? He was the one ready to pop something. Although *that* problem was quickly correcting itself.

"Dani." Pushing out of bed, he walked to the bathroom door and leaned against it. "Dani," he called out louder, and the volume of water on the other side of the door rose proportionately.

"Damn it." He flexed his neck, his left shoulder. "You have to come out sometime."

She didn't answer. He waited another couple of minutes, then blowing out a frustrated breath, he ambled over to the desk and picked up the room service menu. She had to be hungry by now. He was. Or at least he had been.

He took a few minutes to peruse the sandwich selections, and still the water blasted, and still she made no attempt to communicate. After making his decision, he knocked at the door and said, "I'm calling room service. Want anything?"

As irritated as he was, he grinned when the water promptly shut off. After a brief silence, the door clicked open. It inched wider and she poked a wary face through the narrow opening. "Do they have mahimahi sandwiches?"

"Yup. With Maui chips."

Moistening her lips, she shoved the door the rest of the way open. "Okay, but tell them to hold the tomato and tartar sauce." She stepped into the room. "Oh, and I'd like mustard with the chips."

He grimaced, but nodded. "Dessert?"

She pursed her lips in thought, and he picked up the phone and punched in the room service extension while he waited for her answer.

When the attendant answered in three rings, Jack took that as a good sign. He motioned Dani to hurry, then started to place their order.

Dani decided on no dessert and returned his answer by shaking her head. No telling what sugar would do to her already jangled nerves.

Jack was strangely silent as he listened to the person on the other end of the line, yet she knew he hadn't finished giving their order. Keeping her ears tuned to him, she walked to the sliding glass door and gazed out over the mess that used to be miles of beautiful sandy beach.

Debris continued to fly everywhere. Fallen tree limbs

and colorful strips of torn sails were wedged in the most disparate places. Thanks to the ferocity of the wind, part of a boat's splintered propeller had anchored itself into the sand where a stray shell or budding sand castle should have been.

Besides the trash and reminders of such tragic personal loss, it broke her heart to see so much of the pristine beach eroded. Although she'd experienced only one other storm of this magnitude, she knew it would take years before the sand would be replenished, the shoreline restored.

The sight was humbling, and it made her problems seem petty. Until she turned around and looked at Jack again.

He was watching her with such dark intensity that her breath stuttered in her lungs. He recradled the phone but his gaze lingered on her face, the desire in his eyes so blatant that she grabbed the back of the cane-back desk chair for support.

Finally he dragged his gaze past her, beyond the glass doors toward the ravaged beach. "They can't do room service."

"I don't understand."

"Apparently, the entire hotel is operating with half the normal staff and the employees who are here are only available because they can't get home. Besides being stretched thin, they're all working double shifts. Not to mention that the food supplies are dwindling."

"Do they need help? I know my way around the kitchen." Then she added wryly, "I've even made a bed or two."

He smiled. "You're really something, you know that?"

"Why?" Although she detected no sarcasm, she couldn't read his expression, either.

"Most people would be worried about how all this was going to inconvenience them."

She shrugged off the roundabout compliment. "That wouldn't do much good."

"No," he agreed. "And although you didn't ask, how they're handling meals is by setting up buffets in the lounge off the lobby and in the small ballroom. Other than that, they're offering limited menu service in the casual dining restaurant."

"Well, so much for that. I guess I'll raid the minibar. Any more chocolate bars left?"

He laughed. "We don't have to go to that extreme. While we don't have Sam to worry about, let's run down and grab something from the buffet."

Cocking her head to the side, she gave him a skeptical look. "Together? I don't think so."

"I do," he said, his tone stern, his expression implacable. "And this time we *are* going to talk."

IF JACK WAS NERVOUS, he didn't show it as they stopped at the desk to see if the elusive concierge, Carla, was anywhere to be found. Dani on the other hand was ready to jump out of her skin every time someone said something over her shoulder.

After several shrugs and puzzled glances from two exhausted-looking desk clerks concerning Carla's whereabouts, Jack and Dani made their way through the crowded lobby to the lounge. It felt weird to be out in public with Jack, and a couple of times he automatically reached for her hand. Dani was glad she still had enough good sense left to keep it out of his reach.

As sloppily as she was dressed in her two-sizes-too

large T-shirt and long baggy fleece shorts, she was glad to see that others in the buffet line were dressed even more strangely. One woman wore a short kimono-style robe over sweatpants, while a man, laden with gold chains around his neck, had on a gaping floral vest without a shirt, his folded hands resting on his hairy paunch.

Shuddering, she turned away and eyed the long table of food. Considering the circumstances, the kitchen had set out quite an assortment of fresh fruit, cold meats, salads and fancy desserts. Too bad her appetite had taken off as fast as the last gust of wind.

She forked a couple of pieces of pineapple and cantaloupe onto her plate, then added a chocolate éclair. Glancing over her shoulder to satisfy her paranoia, she wandered over to an empty table hoping to put some distance between her and Jack.

Although she didn't know why she should be so worried about getting caught with him. He certainly didn't seem overly concerned. But as she laid her napkin across her lap and searched over everyone's head for him, she noticed that he did a quick survey of the room before coming to take the chair opposite her.

"Is that all you took? I thought you were hungry." He unwrapped his silverware from the linen napkin and looked from his overburdened plate to hers.

She glanced around, feeling her appetite dwindle another notch. "Maybe we can take this up to the room."

His eyes met hers. They were a warm fuzzy shade of brown that told her he appreciated her concern. "Relax. If anyone comes up to talk, you let me handle it. We're just two friends having lunch." He laughed, and she didn't miss the tinny ring of irony in the sound. "Which is the absolute truth."

"You're right." She forced a smile and pierced a chunk of pineapple with her fork.

"Remember," he said, pitching his voice lower. "We haven't done anything wrong."

"Well, not exactly."

"We haven't," he insisted and laid down his fork. "And that's what I want to talk to you about."

He was using that serious tone again, the one that warned her that she might not want to hear what he had to say. She laid down her fork, too. There was suddenly nothing left of her appetite to salvage.

With her napkin, she dabbed nervously at her mouth, and at the same time, she skimmed the room. "Here? Now?"

"Trust me, this is the perfect time."

Her gaze snagged on something bright, neon almost, and relief welled in the pit of her stomach. "There's Mona. She can sit with us. We won't look so *together* that way."

"No. Not now—"

Ignoring him, Dani waved until her mother saw them and hurried over in their direction.

The caftan she was wearing was similar to the one she wore yesterday, except this one was bright orangy red and it was hard to tell where the neckline stopped and her hair began. She looked like a small ball of fire hurling toward them, and Dani didn't even see the Bloody Mary in her hand until she got near the table.

Briefly Dani wondered where Mona had got the change of clothes but she knew better than to ask. Besides not being in the mood for the inevitable long story, she probably didn't want to know.

"What *is* that awful shirt you're wearing?" Mona asked in a voice louder than necessary. Her face was flushed nearly the shade of her drink, and too late, Dani realized it might not have been a good idea to flag her down.

"I don't have a lot of choice," she said in a low voice to give her mother the hint.

"Don't forget about the dress," Jack whispered as he got up to pull out a chair for Mona.

Right. As if she could. Dani snatched up her fork and shoveled a scoop of the rich chocolate éclair into her mouth. Maybe it couldn't cure cancer but it was just what she needed at the moment.

Mona beamed at Jack as she took her seat. "You're going to make a wonderful son-in-law."

Dani choked, and the cure-all chocolate lodged somewhere between her tonsils and her chest. She grabbed blindly for her water.

Grinning, Jack handed her his. "What did you say, Mona?"

Dani coughed. Then before anyone could say another word, she spluttered, "She said you're going to make *Babs* a wonderful son-in-law."

Mona smiled. "Where's the little one? Sam, isn't it?"

Jack took his sweet time dragging his amused look away from Dani. "A friend is watching him."

Mona thoughtfully sipped her drink. "Your friend, does he have dark hair—tall, good-looking?"

He shrugged. "Yeah."

"And his wife has blondish hair?"

Frowning, he said, "He doesn't have a wife."

"Well, she was holding the baby." Lifting a shoulder, Mona fished the celery stalk out of her drink. "Maybe she's the baby's mother."

"Where?" Jack and Dani barked at the same time.

Mona jumped. The celery fell back into the drink, the tomato juice splashing over the side of the glass and onto her hand. "I think that was the same baby I saw. Sam has reddish hair, right?" She peered at them from under her thick false lashes while licking the spill off her fingers.

Shaking their heads and leaning back, they exchanged disappointed glances.

"Hmmm." Mona frowned. "Why didn't you ask me to watch him? I did offer."

"It was a last minute thing. We hadn't had much sleep and..." Jack's gaze met Dani's, and at her thunderous look he stopped in his tracks.

"Would you like me to watch him tonight?" Mona asked, grinning. "So that you two can get some sleep?"

"No," Jack nearly shouted, and Dani stared at him in surprise. "I mean, we're okay. We don't have any plans."

Mona's drink stopped midway to her lips and, frowning, she looked from Jack to Dani. "Not according to the stars."

Dani sighed audibly, then quickly changed the subject. "Did you sleep all right, Mother?"

"Marvy." Her expression softened, her orange tinted lips curving into a coy smile. "I met the most—"

"Okay, we get the picture." Dani eyed her mother's rapidly dwindling drink. "Why don't you have something to eat with us?"

"Oh, no, if I'm not going to baby-sit for you, I'll go rest up for the party."

"What party?" Dani asked automatically, and immediately regretted it.

Jack started coughing and tried to grab his glass, but he backhanded it instead and sent water spraying across the table.

Dani and Mona both pushed back in their chairs, and managed to avoid the bulk of the water, while he quickly righted the glass.

"Sorry," he mumbled, and Dani narrowed her eyes on him.

Something was wrong. He'd recovered remarkably fast from his coughing fit, but his face lacked its usual color. His eyes briefly met hers and there was a wary gleam there which heightened her unease.

Clearly sensing her curiosity, he blinked and shifted his attention. He idly gazed about for a moment, then someone or something apparently snagged his attention because he cocked his head to the side for a better look over her shoulder.

"Would you excuse me a minute?" He flashed them a quick smile, threw his napkin on the table and jumped out of his chair.

Fighting the urge to see where he was going, Dani smiled at her mother. Under raised eyebrows, Mona smiled back. Then slurped the rest of her drink through the straw.

Oh, hell.

Dani turned her head and while pretending to check out the buffet table, she saw Jack shake hands with a slim, distinguished-looking man about Mona's age. Jack flicked a glance her way and quickly she swung back around.

Mona straightened, the interest in her green eyes shining through narrow slits. "Who's that?"

"I don't know."

"We can change that." She fluffed out her hair.

"Isn't he too old for you?" Dani asked blandly.

"Definitely. But he looks like he has money, which is a very nice trade-off."

"Mona." Dani reached across the table and covered her hand. "Don't, please."

She relaxed against her chair back, studying her daughter with keen interest. She withdrew her hand from under Dani's. About to pull hers back, Dani was surprised when Mona switched positions and laid her palm across Dani's knuckles. She squeezed gently.

"Okay," she said, then put both palms up in surrender. "I'll be on my best behavior."

Dani released the breath she hadn't realized she was holding and shakily smiled her thanks. Then she realized she'd probably done more harm than good by asking her mother to tone it down. Generally, she blew off her mother's eccentric behavior. Mona must really be inquisitive now.

"You really like him, huh?" Mona asked.

Resigned, Dani laughed humorlessly to herself. "Yeah, I do. And I don't want to see anything mess up his wedding."

"What should mess it up?" Her mother shrugged, but a shrewd gleam crept into her eyes. "You haven't done anything wrong, have you?"

"No," Dani said quickly. "No, we haven't. Jack isn't like that. He's been very honorable."

Their kiss flitted through her mind, but she dismissed it. It had been impulsive, almost a reflex, but they hadn't allowed it to go anywhere. Although Jack liked teasing her, he had behaved, even when she'd been tempted not to.

"And he hasn't lied to me," she continued. "He told me about his fiancée...about everything from the start.

Jack's a good guy, Mom. I like him. I don't want him to get hurt.''

Hell. Jack arrived at the table just in time to wish he had stayed away one minute longer. He'd heard what Dani said, and now he felt like a bigger heel than he had five minutes ago. But what could he have done? Not only did he have to cancel his drink date with the Brewsters, but if he'd had let his future father-in-law, Danforth Brewster, approach the table he might have said something about the bachelor party in front of Dani.

When Mona looked over her daughter's head at him, signaling his presence, Dani whipped around and gave him a sheepish look.

''Hi,'' he said lamely, feeling pretty sheepish himself. Should he come clean and tell her about the party, or—he groaned inwardly—lie?

''Everything okay?'' Dani asked.

''Fine.'' He sat down, grabbed his fork and attacked his meal. He was shoveling in food he didn't even taste, but at least it bought him time.

''Well,'' Mona said, finally breaking the silence. ''I hear the hotel staff is so worn-out, some of the guests are signing up to help out.''

''Really?'' Dani leaned forward. ''That's very nice. I could probably do that, too.''

Jack swallowed a large chunk of ham without chewing it and nearly choked. ''When?''

Both women looked at him with raised eyebrows.

He shrugged a nonchalant shoulder. ''Now?''

''I don't know.'' Dani frowned at him. ''Maybe tonight.''

He knew it. She *would* choose tonight. ''What about Sam?''

"Can't you watch him? You aren't doing anything, are you?"

"Uh, no." *Damn.*

Dani's eyes narrowed. "Are you sure everything's okay?"

He darted a look at Mona before peering meaningfully at Dani. "Can we talk about this later?"

"Talk about what?"

Mona pushed her chair back, her pale eyes twinkling. "Okay, kids. Time for me to hit the road."

"Wait." Dani blinked. "You don't mean that literally?"

She laughed. "Would I hold out on you, my darling daughter?"

Dani didn't even crack a smile. "What does your rescue worker friend say about the road? Is it still washed out?"

"No change. It's pointless to try and repair it until after the wind dies down. In fact, it's impossible. We're all still stuck here," she said cheerfully and stood.

"Check with me later, okay?" Dani said.

"Maybe you'll change your mind about the party?" she said, her eyes lighting up, and Jack's gut clenched.

Surely there was more than one party going on in the hotel. And she hadn't given him any sly looks. There wouldn't be any reason for her to be invited to the bachelor party or even know about it. So why did he feel so guilty?

"I doubt it," Dani said, laughing. "What kind of party did you say it was?"

Jack managed a strained smile and readied his water glass.

"A cleanup party." Mona raised her empty tumbler to the bartender halfway across the room. The man nodded acknowledgment and picked up a fresh glass and bottle of vodka. Heading in that direction, Mona sighed over her shoulder. "Every young, able-bodied man will be there."

A wry smile tugging at her mouth, Dani shook her head as she watched her mother glide across the room. "Some piece of work, huh?"

"I like her."

Her gaze collided with his. "She's got a good heart. Tough to dig that deep when you're a child, though." She casually lifted a shoulder, but there was a lot of tension in the movement.

"My mom was so normal she was boring."

"Don't knock it." She laughed and seemed to relax.

He leaned forward a little and lowering his voice, he said, "But I know how difficult some parents can make life."

The timing was perfect. He'd been waiting to tell her about Stephanie. Now, not only had she handed him the opportunity, but the setting was right. Although he preferred telling her in private, at least here she wouldn't leave or make a scene before he explained.

"Stephanie's mother can be a little overbearing," he began. "That's the entire reason for this marriage."

He noticed that her features tightened as soon as he said Stephanie's name and he wasn't sure she'd even heard him. Without further thought, he reached for her hand. "Dani?"

"Yo! Dr. Carpenter?"

Dani's chin came up and her eyes met Jack's for one crazy, bewildered second, then she spun toward the voice.

Jack followed her startled gaze. A young man of

about nineteen—blond, tanned, the surfer type—grinned.

"Hey, Dr. Carpenter. I thought it was you. What are you doing here?"

Chapter Thirteen

Doctor? Surely, he'd heard wrong.

Jack watched Dani jump to her feet, and after giving him a brief, apologetic smile, she hurried to meet the young man before he could get to their table.

Under normal circumstances Jack wouldn't consider himself a nosy person, but he'd give up his favorite fishing rod to hear the conversation between those two right now. But not only had Dani waylaid the kid, but she'd smoothly ushered him farther away from the table.

That didn't stop Jack from keeping his eyes on them, though. Maybe he was being touchy, but he thought the young man looked awfully smitten with Dani, leaning close while he talked and laughed. She, on the other hand, looked all business.

Not wanting to look like a jealous lover, Jack forced his attention away from them and stared at his plate. He still had a substantial amount of food in front of him, but he pushed it aside. Who the hell's idea was it to come down here, anyway?

"Sorry about that." She slipped back into her chair and picked up her fork. "Where were we?"

He chuckled. "It sounded like that kid called you 'Dr. Carpenter.'"

She didn't share his amusement. Her gaze roamed his face for a moment, then she broke off part of the éclair that was on her plate and ate it with her fingers.

"Why did he call you doctor?"

"He was in my class last semester." Her tongue darted out to lick the chocolate off her thumb. Then she drew the entire tip into her mouth, her lips pouting around it.

He followed the movement with growing interest until he realized she was purposely trying to distract him. "What do you mean in your class? As in, you were both students?"

She shook her head but didn't look at him.

"You're a...teacher?"

She nodded, pinching off another piece of éclair and studying it.

"Where?" He put his hand over hers, gooey éclair and all.

Her eyes hesitantly rose to his. "The university."

He sank back in his chair, his hand slipping away from hers. "You're a college professor."

"Yes."

"Like in Ph.D....the whole shebang."

"Uh-huh." She shifted and started looking around the room. "Maybe we ought to go get Sam."

"But what about Big Bird?"

She looked him square in the eye. "Not everyone knows about that. I'd prefer to keep it that way, thank you. Now, about Sam?"

"Damn Sam."

Her eyes widened, then narrowed on him. And when

she pursed her lips in disapproval, damn if she didn't sort of *look* like a schoolteacher.

"I didn't mean it like that," he said, "but don't you think we have a little something to talk about here?"

"Nope." She got up and threw her napkin on the table.

"Hey." He quickly signed the check, then shot up and followed her past the bar, through the middle of the buffet line, and out into the lobby.

He didn't mind that she was leaving him in the dust. She had a great pair of legs and an even better backside that was doing exciting things to his thermostat. Even with his big T-shirt covering all the crucial areas, he got a nice glimpse of well-rounded curves. Yup. The view was just fine from where he trotted.

"You're not trying to lose me, are you?" He caught up to her near the elevators.

"I'll pay you back for lunch, by the way. And for dinner last night, too." She touched the *up* arrow and it illuminated. "In fact, Mona might have some money to lend me until I get home."

"I don't care about that. What subject do you teach?"

"Taught." She lifted a shoulder. "But what difference does it make?"

He frowned. "I don't know."

Several people crowded around them, waiting for the elevator, and he moved in close, watching his breath stir the flyaway tendrils around her cheek and neck. She felt it, too, he knew, by the way her shoulders jumped a little and her fingers fluttered to her collarbone.

"What subject, Dr. Carpenter?" he whispered.

"History." Her voice was a breathy wisp and she turned her face a fraction toward his.

"My favorite one."

"Really?"

He smiled when she moved a little closer. "Uh-huh."

She sighed, and he briefly closed his eyes, inhaling the soft feminine sound, the light floral scent that surrounded her.

The elevator dinged. When the doors slid open, disregarding the others who waited, he hurried inside and pulled her along with him. Finding a corner, he backed into it, and drew her close. As the other guests piled into the car, he slipped an arm around her waist and pulled her into the cradle of his thighs. When she stiffened, he softly blew a stream of warm air down the back of her neck.

"Relax," he whispered. "It's crowded. I'm just trying to make room."

He'd purposely leaned close, his lips nearly grazing yet not quite touching her skin and tiny bumps popped up along her nape. He wondered wryly if she felt what had just popped up on him. He didn't wonder long, though. As people continued pouring into the elevator, she was forced even closer, and he knew by the way her fanny muscles tightened, there was no way she'd missed his arousal.

"Jack." Her voice was low but forceful, almost a growl, as she turned her face so that only he could hear, this new position presenting a perfect profile.

Smiling, he exhaled, his breath caressing her ear.

She snapped her face forward, her ponytail whipping across his cheek.

He had to laugh, thinking about how they had a private room and here he was trying to neck on a crowded elevator.

Obviously she didn't appreciate his mirth. Her elbow shot back and jabbed him in the ribs.

He grunted in surprise, then lightly bit her neck in retaliation.

She moved her leg back to step on his foot, but her buttocks rubbed him intimately instead, and she froze.

Pressing against her and bringing his other arm up to hold her more firmly in place, he whispered in her ear, "Stop it some more."

A lady with bleached hair and black roots, wearing too much gardenia perfume, turned and gave him a dirty look.

He winked, and the almost blonde promptly faced the front of the car. Dani's gaze drew to the woman's quick action, then she angled the other way, and over her shoulder asked through clenched teeth, "What did you do?"

"You really want to know?"

She jabbed him in the ribs again.

He chuckled, tightening his hold, and glanced at the tempting expanse of smooth neck as she bowed her head. He wanted another taste but he knew she wouldn't appreciate his forwardness. Not when she hadn't heard his entire explanation yet.

As soon as the car approached their floor, she started to pull away.

He wouldn't loosen his arms. "Let's ride to the top."

"Excuse me," she called out. "Coming through."

He promptly released her when several heads turned and people began stepping aside. Ducking past the sour-faced blonde, he hustled out to the corridor behind Dani.

She didn't wait for him, and not only did he not expect her to, but he was glad she didn't. His jeans had gotten rather snug and it was going to take a moment for him to get comfortable again.

He purposely slackened his steps, giving her a head start, but halfway to the room, the elevator doors clanged shut, severing their audience, and she spun on him.

"What has gotten into you?" Her cheeks were the color of plump ripe strawberries as she continued to walk backward, glaring at him.

"You don't want to know," he said, trying his damnedest to walk normally.

She folded her arms across her chest. "Try me."

"Uh, better watch where you're going."

She stopped, continuing to face him, and her foot started tapping.

He knew the exact second that she recognized something was wrong. She blinked, and her gaze dropped to his feet. Identifying no reason for his limp, her gaze traveled up. When she reached his thighs, her foot stopped, her eyes widened the slightest fraction.

Quickly, she uncrossed her arms and whirled in the direction of the room.

Hell, he'd tried to warn her in a roundabout way.

She got to the room and slid her key card in the lock, opened the door and scooted inside without a backward glance.

He followed, starting to feel a little more normal…and a lot more frustrated.

She had a funny look on her face when he entered and found her staring vacantly at the wall. Her gaze flicked to him and she answered his frown with one of her own.

"I don't even know why I came back here," she said.

"To finish our talk, Dr. Carpenter." He threw his key on the dresser.

"Don't call me that."

"Why not? You earned it. Even though you'd rather dress up like a bird and scare the devil out of unsuspecting men by delivering babies to them," he teased, but her features remained guarded and she said nothing.

"I don't understand you," he persisted. "You act like there's something wrong with teaching."

"Not at all." She pinched the hem of her shirt and kept picking at it until it bunched into her fist. "It was simply time to move on."

Her tone was clipped and he knew he'd better tread lightly. But she obviously had a whopper of a story. You didn't spend years of sweat earning your credentials, then casually decide to move on. Unless you were running away from something.

He frowned when an unpleasant thought struck. "I'd like to hear about it," he said in a casual voice.

She shook her head. "Nothing to tell."

"Do you still teach at all?"

"Are you still getting married?" she snapped.

"Yes."

Color drained from her face and she turned to look out the sliding glass door. "I'm sorry."

"No. I'm the one who's sorry." He scrubbed at his jaw with his knuckles. "I behaved like a lunatic in the elevator without telling you the truth. No wonder you're edgy."

She cast him a sidelong glance but didn't move.

"Other than a very long, platonic friendship, there is nothing between Stephanie and me. Nor will there ever be. This marriage is nothing more than a favor to her."

There, he said it. He took a deep breath as her face, clouded with uncertainty turned toward him.

"Stephanie will tell you the same thing when she gets here." He rubbed his eyes and muttered, "If she doesn't shoot me instead."

Removing his hand, he saw the wariness grow in her eyes. "That's the truth. But you can't breathe a word of this to anyone. Not even Mona. Promise me, Dani."

She moistened her lips. "Of course I won't."

Flexing a shoulder, he went to stand beside her at the glass door. Careful not to touch her, he kept his gaze focused on the raging ocean. "I think this storm is an omen." Sadly, he shook his head. "Bogus or not, this wedding is not meant to be."

"Then why are you doing it?"

"For her family, mostly her mother. It's a complicated story. Because of money and status and a bunch of other crap, Stephanie has been getting a lot of pressure to get married. Especially since her younger sister Bentley tied the knot." He shrugged. "I hadn't seen Steph for about five years when she came to visit me in Brazil last year. She was trying to get away from Babs." He laughed without humor. "Steph's favorite pastime."

"And that's when you two came up with this plan?"

"Not me." He threw up his hands in surrender. "I thought she was kidding at first. And I suppose she probably was. Then one thing led to another and she asked me why I hadn't ever gotten married, and then bingo bango, the next thing I knew I said I'd do it."

He sighed loudly, and with a reassuring hand, she touched his arm. He looked at her then, and a brief smile curved her lips before her fingers skittered away.

The corners of his mouth automatically lifted in response. "To be perfectly honest, I never thought it would come to this. I figured everything would blow over because this marriage tug-of-war has been going on with Babs for years." He shook his head. "But then I get this wedding invitation in the mail—"

"You're kidding." Her eyes rounded.

"I am not kidding."

"You got an invitation to your own wedding? That's how you knew?"

"Just about. I mean, it was a mock invitation so that I could approve the date and time, but by then..." He shrugged and massaged the back of his neck. Getting all this off his chest was supposed to be a relief. So why was there a knot of tension the size of Molokai back there? "I couldn't let Stephanie down. Besides, it didn't seem so complicated at the time. Nothing would change. I'd live in Brazil. She'd continue to live in Honolulu."

Giving up on the knot, he dropped his hand. "And then I met you."

He saw her blink several times, watched the convulsive movement at her throat as she swallowed. Her gaze moved to fasten on something outside, her chin dipping slowly.

"So you see, kissing you wasn't like I was cheating on her." He moved his head and still he couldn't meet her eyes. Hooking a finger under her chin, he lifted her face to his. "The thing is, I want to kiss you right now."

Fear mingled with desire in her eyes as she slowly leveled her gaze with his.

"Do you understand what I've told you?" he asked. "Is there anything you want me to clear up?"

A slight crease formed between her brows and she shifted her chin out of reach. "Why you, Jack? Maybe there's something there. Maybe Stephanie really feels—"

He vigorously shook his head and broke in. "No. There's a little more to it. You don't know Babs. Stephanie can't just marry anyone. He has to be of a certain social class. Like I said, it's very complicated."

Her brows shot up. "You're rich?"

He grinned. "My parents are. I do okay."

Her arms crept around her middle and turning away, she hugged herself. For whatever reason, she looked totally betrayed, and suddenly Jack understood.

"We have a lot to learn about one another, huh?" Gently, he trailed the back of his fingers from her shoulder over her shirtsleeve, down her bare arm. The familiar goose bumps made a prompt appearance, reassuring him.

"Nothing's changed, Jack."

His fingers stilled. "What do you mean?"

"You told me yourself no one can know about this, which means, in everyone's eyes you'll be a married man."

"I don't care about everyone else. I'm surprised you do."

"Don't throw this back on me. You're worried about appearances for Stephanie's sake. I understand and respect that. Although I frankly can't say I understand *why* she'd go through this elaborate charade for her mother—"

"Don't judge her because she's not as strong as you are."

"Me? Strong? Where do you get that?"

He hesitated, wondering how wise it would be to voice his suspicion. "You want to get away from your mother, and you go for it. Although I'm not sure it's worth the price."

"I'm not running away from my mother!"

"You quit your teaching job to deliver telegrams. What else are you doing?"

"I'm having a damned midlife crisis, okay?"

"At thirty-one?" He grinned.

Watching the amusement light up his eyes, Dani fumed. She was *not* running away from her mother. And despite what he thought, she was not judgmental. How could she be? As Mona's daughter, she'd spent most of her life *being* judged.

"Look, I really don't want to get into a discussion about this," she said, staring irritably out at the ravaged landscape. "I had my reasons for leaving the university. Besides, we were talking about you."

"Hey." He tugged at her hand, and against her will, she felt that same overwhelming desire to melt into him every time he touched her. "Let's not fight. We should be celebrating."

She still wanted to be upset with him, but despite his words, she heard the trace of sadness in his voice. And she suddenly realized how much it had cost him to betray Stephanie's confidence.

"She doesn't have to know you told me," she said softly, letting him take her hand.

"Yes, she does." A weary smile managed to reach his eyes. "It's only fair."

"Oh, Jack. I bet she cares about you more than you

think.'' How could the woman not care about someone like him? How could any woman? Dani bit her lip. How could she?

He chuckled. ''Sure, she cares. We're like brother and sister. We were next-door neighbors from the time I was five and she was born until I left for college.''

''And you're sure that's all there is between you?''

''Positive. I wouldn't have agreed to marry her if I thought otherwise. I don't play with women that way.'' Dark with sincerity, his eyes unwaveringly met hers.

Dani was lost. She was one second away from melting into a big sloppy puddle at his feet. There could only be one reason why he wasn't married to a stunning woman with whom he had two-point-five kids, a showcase home and a picket fence that was so white it didn't have a smudge on it. It was because he'd been hidden deep in the jungle away from any woman with half a brain.

He was great with Sam. And Jack not only knew how to spell responsibility and respect, but he could pronounce them, too. She couldn't have given him a better sense of humor. And his butt—it was the best she'd ever seen. Not to mention his thighs, chest, arms...

And his kisses. Oh, sweet heaven, his kisses...

Jack gave her a funny look. He waved his hand to get her attention, and she blinked away her daydream.

Clearly misunderstanding her dazed expression, a slow smile eased across his face, and he said, ''I have another way of proving there's nothing romantic between Stephanie and me.''

''Yeah?'' The word came out a whisper but it was the best she could do.

''Come here.'' He drew the hand he'd been holding

to his lips, forcing her to step closer. He kissed one fingertip, and then another. His gaze remained fastened to hers and she was helpless to look away. He trailed tiny kisses down the side of her finger, and he kissed her palm.

His other arm curved around her waist, and he hauled her body up to his.

She threw her head back in order to watch him, and he smiled. It was a confident smile. One that told her he knew what she wanted. There was no question he'd deliver.

Heat bubbled and pooled in her belly as the thoughts spun chaotically in her head. She still had a lot to think about, their relationship hadn't really changed.

But he wasn't giving her any time to consider the situation. After planting one more long kiss in the fleshy part of her palm, he dropped her hand to her side without releasing it. He kept his warm palm pressed against hers, his fingers stretched out, slowly curving around her fingertips until they sank between hers and locked. He didn't grip her tightly, though, but let their arms dangle close to their bodies, their grasp loose.

Her head was still tilted back, almost as though it were suspended on a cloud, and her eyes had drifted closed. But she knew his mouth was descending upon hers when she felt his warm breath touch her chin.

And then his lips and teeth were nipping her jaw, tiny little bites with only a hint of moisture. He traced a path down to her throat, then licked his way back up with only the tip of his tongue. When he returned to her chin, he took another small bite and her brain started shutting down.

She had to stop him, before everything got out of

control, before she couldn't string two thoughts together. And she would, as soon as she could get her head to quit lolling back on her neck. But before she could pull herself together, his hand came up to cup her nape and he pulled her face up to his, lightly brushing his lips against her lower one. Then his mouth slanted across hers, and she suddenly had no room to protest, no air to breathe but his.

In a second, the kiss turned hungry. With an all consuming urgency, he drew her lips into his mouth, suckling them, prying them open. His tongue thrust between the seam, deep inside, until her knees started to buckle. Before she could recover, or even catch her breath, he pulled her hard against him, his arousal pressing her belly, and chasing away the last of her good sense.

Feeling weak and powerful, lethargic and excited, she lifted a hand to curve around his neck, leaving only a thin cotton barrier between their bodies. Crowning breasts that were tight, aching, her nipples beaded against him.

His tongue slowed and as it receded a little she felt his ragged breath, heard its irregular rhythm. He pressed his lips hard, hungrily against hers once more, then drew back.

"Tell me, Dani," he whispered hoarsely. "Would a man who loved someone else kiss you like that?"

Numbly, she shook her head. Dani honestly didn't know about other men.

She only knew that Jack couldn't.

Chapter Fourteen

When the knock at the door sounded, Jack was tempted to ignore it. No doubt it was Rik bringing back Sam. And then Jack remembered the bachelor party and the fact that he had yet to say anything to Dani.

Reluctantly, he loosened his arm from around her waist and pulled farther back. Her eyes were glazed and bewildered and he was sure his didn't look any different. They had just crossed a threshold and had somehow landed on another plane, some sort of new dimension. He just wasn't sure what the transformation meant.

He cleared his throat. "Dani?"

"You'd better get that," she said, blinking away the confusion. "I think whoever it is has been there awhile."

"Right." He nodded distractedly, and just as the pounding turned insistent, he opened the door.

"You're back." Rik was out of breath. Sam's face was red and tearstained.

"What's wrong with Sam?" Jack reached for him, but the baby turned his face into Rik's shoulder, sending a direct arrow of guilt through Jack's heart. He should've been watching Sam, not moving in on Dani.

"Come on, sport. Don't you wanna come to your Uncle Jack?"

From the protection of Rik's shoulder, Sam eyed Jack peevishly.

"He's out of diapers and I think he's ready for a nap." Rik drew Sam away from him, and tucking his chin down, studied the baby for a moment. "He's okay. I tried to keep him awake as long as I could so he'd sleep through the party tonight."

Jack quickly stepped out into the corridor and let the door close behind him. When Rik frowned, he said, "I haven't asked Dani to watch him yet. She doesn't know about the bachelor party."

Rik's expression turned thoughtful. "You don't think she'll mind, do you?"

"Nah. But I want her to hear about it from me. She *is* doing me a favor by watching this little guy here." Jack wiggled Sam's hand, and grinned when the baby laughed.

"Some girlfriends really hate those stag parties," Rik said.

Staring idly at Sam, Jack snorted. "Yeah. I know." He looked into his friend's amused face. "Shut up, Austin."

"What?"

He shifted his feet, not sure why the satisfied gleam in Rik's eyes unsettled him so much. "It's not like that with us."

The door behind him opened softly, and when he turned, he met Dani's troubled gaze.

"Is Sam okay?" she asked, her attention flitting to Rik before settling on the child.

"He's fine." Jack took the baby. "You think it's too early to potty train him?"

Her features visibly relaxed and a wan smile tugged at her lips. "Let's let him be a kid for a couple more months."

He grinned, sorry he'd worried her, glad she'd rebounded. She put her hands out for Sam, and after Jack released him he cupped her jaw and winked.

Her eyes widened at Rik before she shuttered them, escaping Jack's touch at the same time. "I'll go change Sam," she murmured, and Jack cursed under his breath.

His gaze made a halting trek to his best man.

Grinning broadly, Rik said, "Why don't you give me a couple more diapers and I'll take him back to my room?"

"No," they both said at the same time, then Dani promptly disappeared into the room.

Jack groaned. "I already told you. It's not what it looks like."

"Hey, I didn't see a thing." Holding up both hands, Rik backed away. "I'll see you in a couple of hours, huh?"

Jack watched his friend leave, wondering why Rik's looking so pleased irritated the stuffing out of him. The fact that his friend had been against Jack's marriage to Stephanie from the start was no secret. And Rik didn't even know the entire story.

Yet Dani did.

The thought didn't help his sudden crummy mood. Rik was his closest friend, he'd even saved Jack's life once, and here he was spilling his guts to a total stranger. Except Dani didn't seem like a stranger. And that was another problem altogether.

Dani had left the door slightly ajar, which was lucky for him since he didn't have his key. Once he stepped inside, he saw that she'd already diapered Sam and was playing with him on the bed.

She was lying on her stomach, Sam was lying on his and they met nose to nose, which Dani was teaching him to rub back and forth.

Jack watched quietly for a moment, a little surprised by the swift departure of his foul mood and the contentment enveloping him. The few times he'd been away from the Amazon in the past few years, he'd been anxious to return. But not now. It felt too good to be here—watching Dani.

She looked up and smiled. "Watch this." Scooping Sam up, she deposited him on the floor next to a chair. Once she'd positioned herself in a cross-legged sitting position on the carpet beside him, she set him on his feet.

Sam hung on to the chair and as wobbly as he was, he stood, batting his free hand in his excitement and coming perilously close to losing his balance.

Fisting his hands, Jack fought the urge to grab him when Sam reeled back in his effort to remain upright. But Dani had kept her hands suspended in a bracketing position, ready to catch him if he fell.

"How about that, huh?" She flashed him a grin, then quickly returned her attention to the baby.

Jack's hands relaxed and he felt a smile ease the tension around his mouth. There was no need for him to worry. He could count on Dani to keep Sam safe. He trusted her. With far more than Sam.

"Has he been holding out on us again?" he asked, crouching down to their level.

"I don't know. But he sure the heck surprised me. He pulled himself up when I sat him on the floor while

I was looking for a diaper." She laughed. "He had quite a time doing it. He may have just learned."

Jack caught Sam as he careened backward as if he'd had one too many shots of tequila at the bar. They both laughed, and Jack, holding him by the armpits, set him straight again.

It was strange to think that the baby had only been in their custody for a little over twenty-four hours. He'd crawled and stood and seemed to be growing up right in front of them. For his mother's sake, Jack hoped the kid had already learned to do these things. It would be a shame if she missed out on some of his firsts this way.

This time when Sam reeled, Dani caught him and sat him down on the carpet away from the chair. "I hope this isn't the first time he's done this. His mother—"

"I know," he broke in and ruffled the baby's downy soft hair. "He looks pretty sturdy. I bet he's been doing this for a while."

He had no idea if that was true, but he knew the small lie was worth the trouble when it curved her lips and brightened her eyes. Moving his hand from Sam, he brushed her cheek with his knuckles. Her skin was as soft as Sam's hair.

Dani briefly closed her eyes and he saw her chest rise and fall with the deep breath she took. Then she shrugged. "It's just that I have a feeling that by the time this is all over, she'll have enough regrets."

"Yeah, I know." He withdrew his hand. He knew something about regret, too. It carved out pieces of your life. It threw you into the past, it consumed your future, and left you in such a tailspin that it managed to teach few lessons.

Watching Sam punch excitedly into the air, Jack knew he'd just added another regret to his list. He wasn't going to see the kid take his first step, hear him say his first word. In a few days, he wasn't going to see the kid anymore, period.

So why did he care? He barely knew this child.

And then it hit him. This wasn't simply about Sam. It was about the child he was never going to have.

Jack stared at each of Sam's tiny fragile fingers. Then his gaze drifted down to his toes—teeny little stubs that looked scarcely strong enough to hold up his pudgy body.

Would Sam ever throw a football? Run down the field to catch the winning pass? Would his father coach his Little League games?

Jack wanted those things for Sam, he realized, as icy fingers of need clenched his insides. He wanted them for himself. He was closer to forty than to freedom, if he could even think of his earlier existence that way anymore. Yet, what could he say about his life? Where was it headed?

To the altar.

The sudden thought chilled him as if it were brand-new. The commitment wasn't what frightened him. It was the lie. Could he and Stephanie grow to love one another? Would they ever have a family?

Except it wasn't Stephanie he saw pulling the red wagon, pushing the inner-tube swing. In his mind's eye, a long dark ponytail swung in the breeze.

Dani laughed lustily at something Sam did.

Jack realized he'd been staring at her and he blinked. "Take your hair down."

Her laughter died as she switched her gaze from Sam

to him, then she laughed again, the sound brief and confused. "What?"

"You never wear your hair down."

"I do all the time. Besides, you can't say that. You've only known me for—" she looked at her watch "—thirty hours." When her lashes lifted, her surprise mirrored his.

"I know," he said, nodding wryly. "Seems longer."

"Yeah, like half a lifetime."

He raised a brow at the face she made. "I'm offended."

She exhaled loudly. "This has been a...strange experience."

"No kidding. At this point, I know you better than I do Stephanie."

She laughed, the sound shaky.

He frowned as the truth sank in. "I don't know her dreams, her goals—other than to get her mother off her back." When a guarded look crossed Dani's face, a fresh wave of frustration broke over him. He'd always felt sorry for Stephanie and Bentley with Babs being the pain in the butt that she was. But right now he couldn't seem to summon the usual sympathy. "And I know you're a lot stronger than Stephanie."

"Don't compare us. It isn't fair."

And a lot less self-absorbed, he added silently. Hoping to recapture a lighter mood, he made a face and said, "I don't even know whether she likes mustard with her chips." That got a wan smile out of her. "I also don't know if she likes kids. I even know your favorite color is blue."

"Mustard works with french fries, too," she said, before falling into a thoughtful silence. Then she asked, "How do you know I like blue?"

"You always choose the same color. Both the T-shirts you borrowed and Sam's first makeshift diaper."

"Oh."

She studied her nails for a moment, before glancing up and saying, "About liking kids, I thought you..." Biting her lip, her gaze abruptly returned to her hand. "Never mind."

"No, Dani. I know what you're thinking. Kids were never part of the deal. Just like intimacy isn't."

"I shouldn't have asked."

"It's important to me that you understand. I want you to feel free to ask me anything."

"No. I meant...I didn't need to ask because I know you, too. You wouldn't have led me on." Her eyes were clear and green and so sincere they made him want to square his shoulders, sit a little taller, maybe slay a dragon or two just to be worthy of the respect he saw there.

"No. And I won't hurt you." *I might lie to you about the bachelor party,* he thought grimly, *but I wouldn't deliberately harm you.*

"I know that, too. Just don't ask me how." She turned to stop Sam from crawling away. "I know you're a caring, honorable person who will go out of his way to help a friend. And I know that you still miss football."

"I do not miss—" Frustration returned full force at the smug grin she aimed at him. "What?"

She stared pointedly at the battered shirt he wore. "You have three old jerseys that must be over fifteen years old, two of which should have hit the rag bin ten years ago. You unconsciously polish your ring once every three hours. You—"

"Okay, okay, Miss Know-it-all." Jack frowned, not

sure if he liked this turn of events. "What else do you think you know about me?"

The smile wavered on her lips, and before she could disguise it, a brief sadness dulled the vivid green of her beautiful eyes. "I know that no matter what happens, you'll still marry Stephanie."

"YOU'RE SURE YOU don't mind watching Sam?"

"Jack, would you just leave? You've asked me that three times now." Dani's eyes rolled toward the ceiling as her shoulders sagged in mock exasperation. "Of course I don't mind watching him. And you can be gone longer than half an hour. It's important that you meet with your future in-laws, or they'll start getting suspicious."

Jack made a face as he finished tucking in his shirt. His cheeks looked a little pink in spite of his tan, and not for the first time, she felt a little sorry for him. She knew he didn't care for Stephanie's mother and it was obvious he wasn't looking forward to this meeting.

She watched him search for his wallet, then slip it into the back pocket of his khaki slacks. He patted his smooth jaw as if trying to remember if he'd shaved or not.

The scene was horribly domestic and quite unsettling, but she smiled anyway as he slipped his stockinged feet into a pair of brown loafers, then she said, "You look nice."

"Really?" His forehead puckered in a frown. "Well, I figured I'd better clean up my act. You know, for Babs's sake. I wasn't trying to look *nice,* per se."

She laughed. "There's nothing wrong with looking nice."

She walked over and fixed his crooked collar. He

smelled clean and a little spicy and she knew he'd used something other than the hotel soap. When her fingers brushed his neck, he angled his head so that her knuckles scraped his jaw, her little finger trailed his lips. Desire sprang into his eyes and his breath seared her hand.

She quickly withdrew it. "Stephanie is very lucky to have a friend like you. You're even going all out to impress her parents."

"Yeah." He scrubbed at his freshly combed hair, making a mess of it. "Are you sure you don't mind watching Sam?"

She lifted a hand and pointed to the door. "Out!"

"What?"

"Out."

"Okay." He started for the door, then stopped, and strode to the bed to give Sam a pat on the back. "You be good, huh, partner?" After a second, he stooped down, kissed the baby's head and growled in a low voice, "And no girls."

Sam gurgled with laughter.

Dani grinned and pointed to the door.

"Yes, ma'am." He got there in five long strides, made it halfway into the corridor, then said over his shoulder, "I'll call if I'm gone longer than—"

"Goodbye, Jack." Still grinning, she put weight to the door until the lock clicked and she could no longer hear him.

He'd been nervous for the last couple of hours over this meeting, but she knew he'd feel better once he got it over with. Some time to herself wasn't a bad thing, either, she'd decided, moving to the bed. She had a lot to think about. Like what, in heaven's name, was she going to do about Jack?

After plumping two pillows, she crawled in beside Sam, and watched his growing fascination with his feet. While trying to grab his toes, he would kick them out of reach, occasionally looking at her in surprise and making her laugh. He was good company for her. He helped keep her mind off Jack. But of course, if it hadn't been for Sam, she wouldn't be in this mess at all.

Life had been far simpler yesterday when all she had to worry about was getting to an audition on time. Heck, life had even been simpler when all she had to do was figure out if she should give up teaching.

That wasn't quite true and the memory of having to make that decision stung for a second. But she dismissed it, as she always did. The past had no place in her life.

Absently, she flicked on the television but depressed the mute button. She could watch TV for a while or she could play with Sam, but she knew her problem wasn't going to go away and she felt a prick of resentment that Jack had told her about his relationship with Stephanie.

Her course of action, or lack of action, she thought wryly, had been black and white before she learned of their arrangement. Now everything was as clear as pea soup.

But had anything really changed? He was still going to be married. In her book, a married man was off-limits, no matter what his relationship was with his wife.

But he isn't married yet, a small voice chimed in.

Talk about splitting hairs. Sighing, Dani flipped to the next channel. She was about to release the mute button when she heard the knock at the door.

She glanced a the clock. It was nearly eight-thirty. After boxing him in with pillows to assure herself Sam couldn't roll off the bed, she cautiously peered through the peephole.

One blue-eye-pencil-lined eye, complete with false lashes, loomed close.

"Come on in, Mother," she said as she threw open the door. "I thought you went partying."

Mona's red eyebrows arched. "This early?" Her gaze scanned the room. "Where's Jack?"

"He had some business to attend to."

"Really?"

"What does *really* mean?" Dani frowned at the doubtful tone of her mother's voice as she reclaimed her spot on the bed. This time she stayed in a sitting position, curling her legs beneath her.

"Oh, nothing." Mona sat on the small couch and spread out her low-cut lavender caftan, being careful not to wrinkle it. "Don't tell me you're in bed for the night."

"I'm waiting for a weather report. I want to hear if the airport has opened yet."

"How did I ever raise such a boring child?" Mona started to fold her arms, noticed something wrong with her manicure and flicked at her nails instead. "Do you have any orange nail polish?"

"Oh, sure." After deliberately glancing down at Jack's ratty T-shirt, she inclined her head toward the closet. "Right next to my summer wardrobe, my toiletries and all the other good stuff I just happen to have with me. And by the way, I raised myself."

Mona stared at her daughter for a long silent moment. "You were never sassy, Daniella. Staid, predictable, but never insolent. What's wrong?"

She cringed. "I'm sorry. I guess I'm still tired."

Mona shook her head. "What you need is some air." She waved her hand about the room. "It's too—too claustrophobic in here. There's so much excitement outside. The stars are going nuts with this wind. It almost feels like a blue moon."

Dani nodded patiently. It was pointless to argue.

"Go out for a while. I'll watch Sam."

"Thanks, but I really need to—"

"I insist." Mona reached into her bountiful cleavage and withdrew a folded up bill. "Here's some money. It won't buy much but anything is better than that— that..." She gestured at Jack's T-shirt and frowned. "Maybe you could get one of those wraparound things, a pareau I believe they call it. I'm sure Jack would like to see you in something else besides those rags."

The idea was tempting. Not because of Jack. Well, maybe a little because of Jack. "I don't think so."

"Good. Don't think. That's your problem, Dani. You think far too much." Mona got up and grabbed her daughter's arm, and it was clear by the stubborn look in her eyes that she wasn't going away.

"I don't need anything new. We'll all be able to leave by tomorrow morning."

The wind suddenly howled like it hadn't done for hours, rattling the windows with so much force that even the curtain rod shook.

Mona's eyes widened, not in surprise, but as if she knew something no one else did. She tore her gaze from the window, pulled Dani to her feet, and shoved the money at her. "Take this and go to the boutique before it closes. It's important that you do this now."

Dani knew better than to ask how Mona arrived at this conclusion, so she fisted the money. "You and

Sam stay away from the window, okay? I'll pay you back when I get home.''

"Hurry," Mona said, shooing her toward the door. "And pick out something pretty. Pink goes well with your hair and eyes."

"I won't be long." Dani grabbed her key card off the dresser. "And, Mother, I am sorry about the crack I made earlier."

Shaking her head, Mona waved a dismissive hand. "I know I wasn't always there for you. And sometimes I feel bad about that. Not that I ever wanted to be mother of the year. I just wish I had been more fair to you kids."

Dani started to speak up, not because she disagreed but because she felt an obligation to relieve her mother's guilt.

But Mona stopped her by cupping her chin. "Look at you. You couldn't have turned out any better. Your brothers..." She withdrew her hand to shake it in a so-so manner. "Well, they aren't totally horrible. I won't cry about how I raised you kids, now." She narrowed her gaze, directly meeting Dani's eyes. "Regret is nasty business, you know?"

"Yeah." Dani blinked. "I imagine it is."

Mona nodded sagely. "So, you go have fun. And then would you do me a favor?" She didn't wait for Dani to nod, she merely pushed her toward the door and asked, "Would you stop at the Lanai ballroom on your way back? It's the small one on the ocean side of the second floor. Ask for the banquet captain, Philip."

Dani frowned. "And?"

"Slip on whatever little outfit you buy before you get there."

"Mother, you're *not* fixing me up with this guy."

Mona smiled, the gleam glittering from her eyes so shrewd that it made Dani wince. "The thought never entered my mind."

Chapter Fifteen

Jack took a small sip of his beer and nonchalantly glanced at his watch. Only twenty lousy minutes had passed. Hell, barely half the guests had arrived. At this rate, he was never going to get out of this dump.

His mouth twisted at the thought of that impulsive description. Rik and Jack's future father-in-law, Dan, had gone all out. Despite the fact that the hotel was under a weather attack, Jack noted that the Lanai ballroom was decorated to the hilt. Even the hors d'oeuvres, displayed in long, polished canoes, were color-coordinated, and the two bars were stocked with enough premium booze and pricy champagne to float the entire party to the next island.

"Refill?"

He turned at the sound of the lilting feminine voice, the slight singsong quality identifying the woman as a local. Like the other cocktail waitresses, she was dressed in a short blue-and-cream floral sarong tied around her hips. On top, a scant bra of the same material barely covered her breasts. Her taut brown belly was bare.

She tossed back her waist-long fall of ebony hair,

her knowing smile reaching her sparkling brown eyes. "Your beer? Can I get you a refill?"

Irritated that he'd been staring, Jack promptly mumbled, "No thanks," then turned away.

She was pretty, maybe even beautiful, but that's not why he'd been staring at her, no matter what it seemed like. Upon seeing the woman's silky black hair, his thoughts had quickly strayed to Dani, and how he should be spending this valuable last night with her.

He started to take another sip of his beer, but when he saw Rik walking away from a group of men, he hurried toward him, setting his half-full glass on a table along the way.

"Rik," he called out before his friend could engage in another conversation. As soon as he snagged his attention, and got close enough not be overheard by anyone else, Jack said in a low voice, "I need to get out of here."

"No way." His best man reared his head back, clearly appalled at the idea. "We haven't even got to the best part yet."

"Oh, man." Jack gritted his teeth with dread. "I told you nothing or no one naked."

"I'm not saying a word. I'm not ruining the surprise."

"Yeah, well, I've got one for you, too." He swiveled toward the door...and freedom.

"Jack, I have someone I want you to meet."

Dan Brewster clapped him on the back before he could take another step. Squashing the urge to punch something, Jack forced a smile across his face and turned to his almost father-in-law.

"Jack, this is Carter DeHaven, Bentley's husband,"

Dan was saying as he gestured to the man beside him, who was about Jack's height but younger.

The thought struck Jack that this guy not only didn't look like a Carter, but he didn't look like someone Babs would have picked out for Bentley, either. He liked the guy immediately.

Shaking the man's hand, he realized he liked the way his old friend's husband did that, too. "So you're the one who caught Bentley. Good for you. She's a remarkable girl."

Carter smiled. "I think so, too."

Making small talk for a few minutes, they realized they knew someone in common and as glad as Jack was that Bentley had found such a seemingly good guy, he was anxious to break away and get the hell out of here.

For whatever reason, he sensed Carter wanted to do the same thing, and when the other man excused himself, Jack grabbed the opportunity to break away from the small group. Casually, he meandered toward the bar, noting that the room was filling up. He had no idea who most of these men were, which was a good thing because that would make it easier for him to make his escape.

After stopping briefly to exchange a few words with someone he vaguely recognized, he ducked under the potted palm near the portable bar and quietly asked the bartender for a plain Coke. He knew walking around empty-handed was asking for trouble, yet he needed all his wits about him to make a clean getaway.

The young man poured the cola into a highball glass and topped it off with a lime. Smiling, Jack glanced from the alcoholic-looking drink to the man's name tag.

"Thanks, Kimo."

"No problem." The bartender grinned and handed him the drink. "And congratulations."

"Yeah, thanks." He felt like he was in a damn fishbowl. Everyone knew who he was. But he didn't know spit. He eyed the exit once more. In the good old days, he could sprint that distance in five seconds and not even break a sweat.

"There's another one over there." Kimo pointed toward an obscure door that nearly blended in with the wall. "It goes back to the kitchen, but there isn't much staff around to notice if you use it."

Jack squinted at the man. Although Kimo was still grinning, he'd already moved on to the next person's drink.

Jack exhaled sharply, raking a hand roughly through his hair. Hell, was he that obvious?

"Can I have everyone's attention?" Rik's voice rose above the hum of the party, and everyone looked his way. His gaze skimmed the crowd. "Would the man of the hour step up here, please?"

Pair after pair of eyes turned toward Jack.

He muttered a curse and downed his drink. As he placed the empty glass on the bar, Kimo said, "You shoulda made a run for it."

"No kidding." Jack murmured one last choice word for good measure and scrounging up a smile, headed toward his friend.

At the same time, the employees' door opened and a gigantic cake was wheeled out by three scantily clad cocktail waitresses.

"Oh, no." Jack looked at the wide grin on Rik's face and for the first time that he could remember, he seriously wanted to punch his friend right in the kisser.

"Come here, Jack." Rik advanced.

The waitresses, and miles of cleavage, also advanced with the cake. As they did, the top of the frilly confection shook free, flicking white frosting in all directions. Within seconds, a blond head appeared, followed by a pair of bare shoulders.

Somewhere near Rik, a drink crashed to the floor. Someone uttered an earthy curse. It sounded a lot like Jack's best man.

The waitress who had asked Jack if he wanted a drink earlier, stepped up and wrapped her long brown fingers around his arm, urging him toward the cake. Her smile beckoned, her wink was seductive.

Reflexively, Jack cast a quick, longing look at the other door.

And felt his jaw drop a foot.

"Dani?"

Clearly taken aback, shock radiated from her like a sonar blast. Her face turned as pink as the brief floral dress she wore. And even from where he stood, he could see the confusion darken her eyes to mossy green as she started to back out of the room.

Guilt dealt a swift and exact blow, and for a moment, he couldn't move.

You lied to her, pal. Proud of yourself?

"Damn it." He forced his feet to move just as the lights flickered once, twice.

The wind screeched, shaking the building.

And then everything went black.

DANI GRIPPED the door frame, anchoring herself while she sought her bearings in the dark. Although it wasn't the sudden inky blackness that unsettled her, that made her need to hold on to something until her knees no longer felt as unsteady as chocolate pudding.

It was the sight of Jack that had hurled her into shock, that had made that same jolt dissolve into hurt so deep it made her teeth ache.

She swallowed around the pain, and when simple, liberating anger began to fill her, she inhaled deeply with gratitude.

He had lied. And what irked her the most was that it had been a petty, needless lie…unless it had been meant to manipulate.

Anger exploded anew as she felt her way along the wall, down the corridor toward the stairwell. Already people had rushed out of the ballrooms and were pouring blindly into the hall, their presence heralded by panicked murmurings.

Raised voices from the hotel staff urged everyone to stay calm as they distributed candles. Several small flickers of light bobbed through the darkness, their numbers growing as wicks touched and candles were passed around.

Although Dani didn't yet have one, there was enough light for her to safely make it to the stairwell door. She paused briefly when she thought she heard Jack calling her name. Not because she had any intention of waiting for him to catch up, or because she wanted to talk to him at all, but because, sadly, when she'd heard his voice, she'd waited instinctively.

And with anticipation, she realized in a sudden extra dose of anger.

Someone handed her a candle just as she slapped the door open. People were behind her, waiting to enter the stairwell, so she plowed ahead as quickly as safety would permit.

By the time she'd maneuvered five flights of stairs, she was barely breathing hard. Adrenaline propelled her forward, her thoughts a mad tangle of irritation and self-reproach.

To him she was obviously just a baby-sitter. A means to an end. Nothing more. He had snapped his fingers and she not only stepped up to the line, she'd made a mad dash.

There was only one thing she despised more than men who used women. And that was the weak women who allowed the contemptible behavior.

When she got to the room, she quietly sagged against the door, trying to regain her composure before having to face Mona. She took deep, calming breaths until the anger and disgust stopped swirling and fluttering in her chest. And for the first time, she felt a spark of sympathy for her mother. She now understood how Mona could be so blissfully stupid, how she could want to believe a man so totally that she was blind to the truth.

At least Dani was lucky. She hadn't yet invested an emotional stake in Jack.

Unlocking the door, she called herself the liar that she was.

The room was black and an eerie feeling crawled into the jumble of emotions that already had her nerves threadbare.

"Mother?"

She lifted the candle to shed some light on the open bathroom door, then swung the flame toward the bed. Sam was nowhere to be seen, and on the nightstand lay the unused candles the hotel staff had delivered yesterday.

Alarm made the flickering ray of light all the more

unsteady as she moved it around the room. Then she saw the sheet of hotel stationery on the coffee table.

She recognized her mother's lazy scrawl as soon as she picked up the note. *Figured you two would want some privacy. Don't worry about Sam.*

Dani blinked. *Why would—*

She laughed, and recognized the bitterness in the sound. Mona was going to be appalled at how far off the mark she was this time. How her plan to hook up Jack and Dani had actually backfired.

Dani shook her head, not missing the irony that it was due to Mona that she'd finally seen the truth. Just in time, too. Only a half hour ago she'd decided not to pass up her one chance to love Jack. But that was before she realized she meant nothing to him. Unlike her mother, Dani wouldn't settle for being a man's convenience. Even Jack's.

JACK SLID HIS KEY CARD into the lock, praying he was right, hoping Dani had returned to the room. As soon as he opened the door, he saw the flickering candlelight coming from the bathroom.

Relief surged through him, and he quietly pulled the door shut behind him. When he heard water running, he hesitated near the open bathroom door.

"Dani?"

The water shut off, leaving a wall of silence between them. He knew she was angry and hurt. He'd seen both emotions steal across her face right before the lights went out. But he didn't know just how much damage he'd caused. If the piercing silence were any indication, he was in deep trouble.

"Dani? I can explain." He inched closer to the door.

She hadn't slammed it. He'd take that to mean she was decent and open to discussion.

"Not necessary." Her tone was flip, indifferent. He didn't like it.

"Can I come in?" he asked.

"That's not necessary, either."

When she came through the door, he blinked. A blur of yellow, she swept past him, carefully holding the lighted candle away from her body and all the bedraggled yellow, polyester feathers.

He laughed. He couldn't help it.

She threw him a quelling look.

He cleared his throat. "Why do you have that Big Stork costume on again?"

"It's Big Bird. And I'm leaving."

"Come on, Dani. I know you're angry and I don't blame you—"

"Your clothes are hanging in the shower. I hand-washed them. Now, kindly get out of my way."

"Damn it, Dani." He stood directly between her and the door, a feeling of déjà vu taunting him. "This isn't at all like you. Please don't—"

"You're wrong," she snapped, and he could tell that he'd pushed a button by the way her eyes flashed with annoyance. "This is exactly like me. What wasn't like me was the way I played doormat for the past day and a half."

"What?" He shook his head, bewildered. "I lied to you. I'm a jerk for doing that. But you were never a doormat."

She sighed, the sound so full of disappointment and resignation that it made his gut twist. "It doesn't matter, Jack. Go have a nice life, okay? And for what it's worth, I'm really still not sorry I met you."

Her smile was faint and sad, and Jack would have preferred that she kneed him in the groin. When she started to step around him, he grabbed her by the shoulders.

"I know you, Dani. You won't walk away without letting me explain. Even if you don't like the explanation." He stared intently at her cool expression. "Because it's the fair thing to do."

She blinked, and in that instant, her features softened. "Watch the feathers."

"What?" His gaze followed hers to his candle, the flame hovering only inches from her costume. "Right." Reluctantly, he broke contact. "Weren't you wearing something else downstairs?"

Before he got the last word out, her expression had tightened again, her gaze drawing to the boutique bag she had clutched in her other hand.

He remembered now. The little dress she'd been wearing was short and pink and sexy, as if she'd been planning to...

"Oh, hell. Dani, we've gotta talk. And I'm not taking no for an answer." He tried to propel her back deeper into the room, but she shook free.

"That's your problem. I bet you never have to take no for an answer. Consider this a lesson learned."

He'd made her angry all over again, that was obvious, and since he was already feeling like the scum of the earth, he figured another infraction wouldn't make a difference.

"Where's Sam?" he asked suddenly, and was relieved to see his ploy work. She stopped in her tracks. Her eyes widened in what seemed like confusion with a hint of sheepishness.

He wasn't really worried. No matter where Sam was,

Jack knew Dani had kept him safe. He was merely buying time. She would never storm off without accounting for the baby.

"I'm not sure," she said, clutching the bag tighter. "Mona has him. They were gone when I got back."

"Did she leave a note?"

She nodded first, then shook her head. "But it doesn't say much. Ouch!" The hand holding the candle jerked. "That wax is hot."

"Here." Jack removed the candle from her hand. He glanced around the room for a moment, then grabbed an empty water glass and stuck both candles inside.

When he looked at her, she was staring at the pair of flames as if transfixed. "It won't do me any good sitting in there."

"After we talk—" Her sharp yet wary glance brought him up short. "About Sam," he added, gently. "You can take the candle—"

"Jack, don't try and manipulate me anymore."

Anymore? He winced inwardly, painfully aware that that was exactly what he was doing now. But anymore?

"Okay," he said. "You're right. Although I am concerned about Sam, I know you wouldn't let anything happen to him and I was using him to keep you here."

Her lips thinned and he mentally recapped his spiel.

"I meant now," he said quickly. "I purposely brought him up because I knew you wouldn't leave without explaining where he was. And I wanted you to stay…so I could explain why I've been such a jerk."

"Okay." Lifting her chin, she crossed her arms. "Why *have* you been such a jerk?"

"Because I didn't have enough—" Stopping himself, he half smiled. "Let's just say that a certain part of my anatomy was sufficiently lacking for me to tell

Rik to go to hell with the bachelor party, or to be honest with you about going.''

''That doesn't tell me anything. Why didn't you explain to me about it beforehand?''

''Because I didn't want you to think that's how I'd choose to spend what's probably our last night together.''

She looked away, the flickering light casting odd shadows on her face and making her expression totally unreadable. He could only hope that she was trying to digest what he'd said. And that she understood.

''I'm sorry that I jumped to a conclusion about how you'd react,'' he said. ''I'd planned on going for less than an hour. Long enough to keep Rik off my back and not breaking the door down looking for me. Then I was going to sneak away and spend the rest of the night kissing and holding you.''

Her gaze swung back to his, and she measured him with undisguised frankness. And then the barest hint of a smile tugged at the corners of her mouth.

''I know that sounds corny and I don't believe I just said that.'' He broke eye contact and sprawled across the small couch. ''Do you mind if I sit while I grovel?'' He scrubbed at his eyes, his hair.

''You can sit,'' she said, her tone clipped. ''As long as you keep groveling.''

Slowly, he met her gaze. She didn't look nearly as stern as she sounded, and her lips were still soft with banked amusement. ''I could get down on my knees. That should help the effect.''

''Honesty would help the effect.''

''I know.''

''You think I'm overreacting, don't you?''

"No." He shook his head, his eyes steadily fastened to hers. "I lied."

"What else have you lied about?"

"Now that I've completely ruined my credibility with you, will you believe me when I say nothing?"

She nibbled at her lower lip. This clearly wasn't a simple decision for her. "I have one more question for you," she said, her expression going totally blank again.

And Jack knew even before he heard the question, that his answer would not be the one she wanted to hear.

"Are you still going to marry Stephanie tomorrow?"

He felt the world slip out from under him and his shoulders sagged against the back of the couch. "Yes," he said. "I am."

Slowly, she nodded. "That's what I thought."

Then she unzipped the front of the Big Bird costume, revealing only a brief blue bikini underneath, and let the feathered concoction fall to the floor.

Chapter Sixteen

Watching shock darken Jack's face, Dani swallowed hard. She hoped he wasn't having second thoughts. She wasn't. Nor did she doubt what he'd told her about his relationship with Stephanie. Her decision to make love with Jack felt right.

That he hadn't been honest about the bachelor party still didn't sit well with her, but in a way she understood, and where it really counted, he'd been brutally honest. Tomorrow, weather permitting, he'd marry Stephanie.

And that's when everything would change irrevocably. No matter what his deal was with his new bride, once he said "I do," Dani wouldn't. But for now, before the vows were exchanged, she could justify this one night. Because like it or not, she'd fallen hard.

At a loss for words, she eyed the forgotten boutique bag containing the short pareau she'd worn for a matter of minutes. As much as she'd like to be wearing it for Jack, she knew she should return it for the cash she'd spent—cash that could well be her ticket out of here come morning.

He cleared his throat and she switched her attention back to him. "This is a little awkward," he said, his gaze briefly traveling the length of her body, his desire so blatant it gave her confidence. "I'm not prepared."

"I am." Ducking from his surprised look, she snatched up the bag. Although it was liberating to admit to her obvious planning, it was also embarrassing and in her unease, she found herself wrestling with the uncooperative plastic.

"Let me." He took the bag from her shaky hands, withdrew the condoms and placed them on the nightstand.

As annoying as it was, she still had trouble meeting his eyes and when she glanced away, she noticed the drooping bouquet of gardenias and ginger on the table in the shadows.

"Those were the best I could do, but they're still pretty fragrant," he said, and she caught a brief glimpse of a smile before he yanked his shirt over his head.

Inhaling deeply, she was amazed that she hadn't noticed them before. "I can smell them from here."

"Really?" he said, draping the shirt over the back of a chair, his unwavering gaze locked with hers. "And what are you doing *way* over there?"

She tried to breathe but her lungs had trouble engaging. Even though she'd seen him without his shirt several times, even though she'd already shared more intimacies than she would have with most men after twenty dates, her nervousness doubled.

She knew why. Tonight was different from the other times. Tonight would be their last together. Everything had to be just right. The memory would be all she had to keep with her. She hoped Jack had a slow hand.

"Are you having second thoughts?" he asked when she didn't answer.

She shook her head. "Are you?"

"Nope. I've had the same thought for about thirty-five hours now."

She made a face, and he grinned.

"Okay, I'm exaggerating," he said, walking toward her and shrugging without apology. "But only because I'm too old to keep thinking like that and not have a heart attack." He stopped and placed his hands on her shoulders. "You're beautiful. What else would I be thinking?"

"Well, you could think about how smart I am." Her muscles tensed under his warm palms, and she suddenly wished that she had on something else besides the bikini top.

"Yes, you are smart," he agreed as he gently kneaded her shoulders. "And caring. And funny. And sincere. And you are one very tense lady. Are you sure you're okay with this?"

When his finger hooked below her chin, Dani realized her eyes had drifted closed. Opening them, she met his concerned gaze and nodded slowly. "Especially this part."

He laughed. "Why don't you lie down and I'll give you a massage like you've never had before."

"That should be easy. This is my first."

"Well then, listen to the master." Circling his hand above her elbow, he led her closer to the bed. "First, we get rid of any obstructions."

Standing behind her as she faced the bed, he unhooked the top of her bikini. She tried not to react, but her tongue darted out to moisten her lips, goose bumps surfaced on her skin and her nipples hardened immediately.

He didn't let the bra fall away, rather he reached

around and drew it across her body, letting first the fabric then his knuckles graze her breasts.

"Uh, do you have any kind of credentials for this?" she asked, trying for levity and sounding breathless and eager.

He chuckled, his breath caressing her skin, and then she got her answer as she felt the warm moist pressure of his lips between her shoulder blades, down her spine, back up again.

She closed her eyes and fisted her empty hands at her waist. It was maddening having him behind her, not seeing his face, not being able to touch him. And though he was barely touching her, too, only his feverish lips skimming her back, her skin was so sensitive that even the damp humid air felt like an embrace.

His hands. She didn't know where his hands were. The sudden thought sent a little shock wave through her.

"You're tensing up again," he whispered, and then his hands were on her, cupping her breasts, kneading them, making her nipples ache with anticipation.

His lips moved along her back, up to her neck, until he nipped at her earlobe. When his tongue traced the shell of her ear, she sagged against him.

His arms tightened around her, crossing above her waist, each hand cupping a breast, her nipples pearling between his fingers.

"I want to make love to you," he whispered, his breath ragged in her ear, before he kissed the side of her neck, the top of her shoulder. Then his hold loosened as he stepped back and slowly turned her around.

She had the fleeting urge to cover her bare breasts as she faced him, but the tenderness in his expression as his gaze touched her hair, her eyes, her mouth, chased any residual doubt from her mind. When his attention finally settled on her nakedness, the hunger that glittered in his eyes made her knees grow weak.

Struggling for composure, she lowered her gaze to his chest. Dark hair shadowed a wedge of his chest between nipples that were beginning to pucker. Candlelight danced and flickered down to his waistband where a mat of hair grew dense before tapering off into his trousers.

"Come here," he said, a smile lifting one corner of his mouth.

A little disconcerted that she'd been so obviously staring, she let him pull her toward him until her breasts flattened against him and her open palms lay splayed across his shoulders. Wrapping an arm around her waist, he held her tightly, briefly closing his eyes and letting a slow groan rumble from his throat.

"You feel so good." He tasted the side of her mouth, trailed a string of fiery kisses along her jawline. And then his mouth covered hers and he parted her lips with his tongue, delving and plunging until she was breathless with wanting him.

When she pulled back to gulp in some air, his mouth left hers to find a breast. And after circling a nipple with his tongue, he took it into his mouth and suckled while one hand did amazing things to the underside of her buttocks.

The other hand he used to keep her flush against him, his desire prodding her, telling her he was ready. But he didn't rush, he didn't push.

And Dani didn't expect him to. After all, this was Jack.

She closed her eyes, breathing in the clean spicy scent of him and dragged a palm from his shoulders over his aroused nipples and down his belly. Her little finger edged beneath his belt and his muscles contracted against her marauding hand. Quickly, he grabbed her wrist.

"Who's tense now?" She smiled into his tortured face.

His eyes narrowed, then crinkled at the corners. "You haven't see anything yet."

Before she knew what was happening, he scooped her up and carried her to the bed, dumping her in the center. It wasn't a rough dumping, but it wasn't too gentle either.

"Is this the Amazon version of 'Me Tarzan, you Jane'?" Her interrupted grin returned at the look of frustrated determination on his face, and she provocatively lifted her rear to the other side of the mattress, lounging, pointing a teasing leg in his direction.

"No, honey." He unbuckled his belt and slid it from the trouser loops. "I don't want any mistaking who I am."

The frustration was gone, burning intensity smoldering in its place as he grabbed her ankle, pulling her to him and eliciting a yelp of surprise from her.

"Jack." The breath left her in one, swift whoosh.

"I knew you'd get it right."

She felt his smile stretch across the sensitive skin below her ear, move to the hollow of her throat, brush her right breast. Reclining beside her, he wrapped one arm around her waist and cupped her bottom.

"I heard something." She stiffened, peering at the closed door, and he slipped a finger under the elastic of her bikini.

"Wind."

"No, inside."

"My heart."

A nervous laugh tickled her throat. She knew he was trying to be funny but she thought he just might be right. Except it was her heart that she heard pounding in her ears as he slipped yet another finger under the elastic and slowly slid the bottoms down her thighs, past her knees. When it got to her ankles, the gentleness vanished and he jerked the bikini off with an impatient yank.

The abrupt action startled her and when she sought the comfort of his reassuring gaze, he turned away. Doubt pricked her confidence, as she watched him reposition a candle. The flame shifted and flickered over her nude body. Jack's jaw tensed, his ravenous gaze following the light, before meeting her eyes and giving her all the reassurance she needed.

"Dani, I have never wanted a woman more than I want you right now." A slow, sexy smile tugged at his sober expression. "And I'm damn glad you happened to come in one helluva nice package."

She looped an arm around his neck and pulled him to her, kissing him with every ounce of passion and strength she possessed. She knew she'd surprised him, but he took no time to recover.

He kissed her back, hard, urgently, while he loosened his pants, then shoved them aside.

Immediately she felt his arousal nudge her, pressing into her flesh, telling her how badly he wanted her. Yet still he didn't rush, but continued to taste and knead and slip his fingers into secret places until she thought she would burst from the pleasure of his slow touch.

Briefly she wondered if he was deliberately taking his time because he, too, knew that this would be their one and only taste of happiness together. Reminded of that glum certainty, she could wait no longer and rolled atop him grabbing the condoms at the same time.

She found him quickly and slid onto his heat before he could stop her. He lifted a weak hand, pushing her hair away from her face, whispering her name. He felt hot and heavy inside her and for a senseless moment, she thought about uttering the words that had teased her consciousness all day.

But it wouldn't be fair to tell him she loved him now, she decided as she sank deeply onto him. Because tomorrow he was marrying someone else.

Chapter Seventeen

The candles had nearly burned down to the glass when Jack finally awoke. Surprised he'd fallen asleep at all, he swung a look at Dani. But she was asleep, too, her nude body curled toward him, her expression totally relaxed. The waning candlelight barely reached her face but it cast enough illumination that he saw the dry tearstains on her cheek.

A large breath imploded painfully in his chest and he had to exhale slowly to keep from jerking upright and disturbing her.

Was she sorry that they'd made love? Had he not gone slowly enough? The first time wasn't his fault, he assured himself, carefully turning onto his side so that he could face her. She hadn't given him any choice. The thought made him smile. It gave him hope.

Maybe they had been happy tears.

Lightly he traced one dry patch with his thumb. He wanted to think he had the guts to ask her, but once she opened those big green eyes, he didn't know what he'd do if he saw the barest hint of regret there.

She mumbled something softly, her eyelashes fluttering. She still didn't open her eyes, though, and he took the extra moment to steel himself for her reaction.

Her hand covered her mouth and she stifled a yawn before starting to lift her lids, blinking, then widening her eyes to meet his.

He took the hand away from her mouth and kissed the tips of her fingers. "Morning," he said with a smile.

"Is it really?" She blinked again before focusing on him. And then her lips lifted into such a beautiful ingenuous smile he knew he'd carry this picture of her in his heart forever.

"I think so. But it's still early yet." He kissed her bare shoulder.

"Hmmm." Her eyes started to drift closed again and then they popped open. "Where's Sam?"

"Still with your mother. She never came back with him."

She frowned.

He raised himself on his elbow. "He's okay, isn't he?"

"Well, yeah, Mona will take good care of him." The frown remained etched in her face as she tried to get out of bed.

He stopped her with a hand on her arm. "What's wrong? Is it about us?"

Her expression softened and she shook her head. "Us was wonderful." She smiled, and his heart expanded. "It's Mona. She's going to think something happened between us."

Jack stared at her. Something happened all right. Something magical. And watching her now familiar face, he knew a spell was being woven again. He didn't know her that well, yet he knew her for a lifetime. That's where the magic took over, replacing logic and doubt, convincing him he was about to do the right thing. He hoped the magic helped Stephanie understand why he couldn't marry her.

Dani was looking at him funny, gathering the sheet to cover her breasts and he knew he'd stared too long without commenting. "Um...it did."

"I know that." She made a funny face. "Mona is just..." Shuddering, she said, "I really don't want to talk about it."

He smiled. She was going to talk about it, all right. She'd given him the perfect opening to discuss their future. "Dani, do you believe in magic?"

She started to laugh, then her eyes narrowed and she looked inexplicably hurt. "No. I don't believe in psychics, astrology, fortune-tellers or palmists. Contrary to your obvious belief, this apple falls very far from the tree."

"What?" He tried to catch her hand. She yanked it away. "You're misunderstanding me."

"Mona's the one with the red hair, remember?"

"Hey, quit being so touchy about your mom long enough for me to explain."

"I'm not touchy about—" She cut herself off with a small self-conscious chuckle. "Okay, maybe I am a little."

Hearing her laugh, tension fled him like the air being let out of a balloon. So much was on the line here. He needed to tell her how he felt about her. He needed to know if she felt the same way.

"Let's not talk about Mona, okay?" he said, and this time he snagged her hand and brought it to his lips.

She sighed as he kissed her palm. "Well, you'll have to put up with it for a few more minutes. There's something I want to make clear to you."

Although he didn't like the serious tone of her voice, he nodded and let her withdraw her hand to clasp the other one in her lap. The sheet she'd wrapped around her sagged with the action and he tried not to let the hollow between her breasts distract him.

"You were wrong about me running away from Mona. Well, maybe you were half-right."

"That doesn't matter, Dani—"

"It does to me. I want you to know." She looked down, studying her hands. They shook a little, then she clasped them so tight her knuckles paled. "This is probably the last time I'll ever see you and I want you to know that I'm not some little coward who's worried about what people think of her or her mother."

"What do you mean the last time?"

"Have you forgotten you're getting married?"

"That's what I want to talk to you about—"

"There's nothing to discuss. If I said I didn't feel some guilt for sleeping with you I'd be a liar. I believe you and Stephanie have only a platonic relationship and that this marriage is supposed to be strictly business, but things could change and I won't come between you. Besides, vows are vows."

He started to grin, anxious to reveal his decision, but she sprang up, grabbed a shirt and slipped it over her head. It was his polo shirt—the one he'd worn last night. She didn't seem to notice.

"You're wrong," he said quickly, losing the grin.

"Anyway, I'm leaving tonight. If all goes well I won't be back to the islands for a year. You'll be long gone. And like I said I'm not leaving because of Mona." She pushed back her hair with an agitated jerking movement. "I'm leaving because of Indiana Jones."

"What?" He laughed. It was an automatic reaction even though dread was skidding down his spine. She ducked her head and he knew she hadn't meant to say that. "What?" he repeated.

"And because of tenure." Her shoulders drooped and when she slanted him a look, she half smiled. "It's a long story but I'd been getting pressure to publish something in order to attain tenure at the university. My life was so exciting that I was watching Indiana Jones on my thirty-first birthday when I realized I hadn't even lived yet. How could I write about anything?" She threw up a hand. "I'd spent so much time worrying about doing the right thing, acting a certain way that I slipped into a career that was practically handed to me. That afternoon, I knew I had to get out."

"Just like that."

"Just like that," she agreed, her eyes seeking his, asking for understanding. "I wasn't sure who I was anymore."

"I understand." And he did. Totally. As much as he wished he didn't, he admitted as the bitter taste of loss coated his mouth and dripped like acid down into his stomach. Because understanding made it too difficult to be selfish. How could he ask her to give up her dreams now?

"I knew you would." She smiled.

It was a special smile. The kind that was meant for only one person. Him.

He felt nobility slip a notch. He could ask her to stay with him. The decision should be hers, he told himself, letting nobility take another dive.

"How?" he asked.

Her lips twitched. "How did I know you would understand?"

He nodded, glad she had so much faith in him, and knew he should leave it at that. This was one of those questions better left unasked because the answer was likely to catapult him into a no-win situation. But the same as when he was a kid and he knew his mother wouldn't extend his curfew, he asked anyway.

"Well, because of our connection," she said, then grimaced. "Not in the mumbo-jumbo sense Mona sees it. I mean, I feel like even though we haven't known each other long, we, uh…we understand each other."

He grinned at the way her cheeks flushed slightly, and because he just damned well felt like it. She sensed the magic, too.

"Gee, great. Now I don't think you understand anything I'm saying." Her hand fluttered in a small gesture of distress. "I meant that maybe you understood because of the football stuff. You know, your running away to the Amazon after football didn't pan out."

His smile vanished. "I didn't run away."

She blinked. "Okay, so I didn't word that correctly."

He stared at the guarded look shuttering her face. "Tell me what you meant."

She shrugged. "What did you call heading for the Amazon?"

"A career shift."

"Okay, that's what I'm doing."

"You implied there was more to my decision."

"I'm sorry if I did. I didn't mean to."

Her eyes were frank and direct and he had not a single doubt that she meant every word she'd just said. But that knowledge didn't lessen the sting. She knew he had run away. Run from a society that wouldn't hail him as a football hero. Run from the fear that he no longer had a worthy identity.

"We're not going to argue during our last few hours together, are we?" Her tone was a little teasing, a little nervous, her green eyes pleading. She knew she had gotten to him. She just didn't know how badly.

"No." Ignoring the pressure building in his chest, he grabbed her hand and drew her to him. He wasn't about to let the past ruin his chance for happiness, even if that happiness was only going to last for a couple of hours. He couldn't ask her to stay now. Not when she'd reminded him of how important leaving can be.

"We're not going to argue," he confirmed with a bittersweet smile. "We're going to make love."

As he gathered her soft, sweet-smelling body in his arms, he couldn't help mentally kicking himself. He knew he shouldn't have asked that damn question. It was enough that she did understand him. He should have had the faith she had.

WHEN THE PHONE RANG an hour later, Dani instinctively knew this was the beginning of the end for her and Jack. And it seemed that she was right—within seconds after he picked up the receiver, power was restored to the hotel, flooding the room with the lamplight that had been left on last night.

The bed was a sorry tangle of sheets and the floral quilt hung gamely from the corner. Clothes lay strewn across the floor, and on the nightstand the gardenias and ginger wilted limply over the side of the glass. In the discerning lamplight, romance and ideals yielded to flaws.

The irony was almost too much for her and she slipped out of bed, pulling a dislodged sheet with her, wrapping it around her body, keenly aware of his watchful eyes. After listening to his side of the conversation for a moment and concluding that it was Mona on the other end calling to say she'd be bringing Sam back, Dani locked herself in the bathroom before Jack could get off the phone.

She turned on the faucet and splashed her face with cold water. As much as she craved a shower, the feel of Jack's warm touch lingered on her skin and she didn't think she could ever willingly wash the sensation away.

Or could mere water even do that? Could it wipe away the feeling of being so thoroughly loved you thought you just might die from it? Water wasn't going to do that, she knew, nor would years of trying to forget. Because the feelings that clawed at her heart had little to do with his touch...and everything to do with the man himself.

Yet he wasn't hers to keep.

She'd lied to him to some degree. She was leaving because of Mona. Not for the same reason he thought, but because Dani had never been so in danger of being like her mother as she was now. She wanted to tell Jack to stay, that she'd agree to any arrangement he wanted, be his weekend lover, go with him to the Amazon. She was close to abandoning every principle she'd ever upheld.

And that sudden weakness scared her to death. Because she knew she couldn't do any of those things without losing a major part of herself.

Reluctantly, she raised her eyes to the mirror. She looked the same. Yet she'd never felt so out of sync in her life. But if she wanted to be able to keep meeting those eyes every morning without cringing, she knew what she had to do.

"Dani?"

Jack's voice was low and strained on the other side of the door.

She took a deep breath. "I'll be right out."

"Can I come in?"

She dabbed at the darkness around her lower lashes but there was nothing she could about it beyond getting a good night's sleep. Not that the odds were very likely.

As she opened the door, she forced a smile. "You can have it all to yourself."

"I wanted us to take a shower together." He reached for her but she slipped past him.

"Isn't Mona coming up?"

"I asked her to give us a half hour."

"Great. She'll have a field day with that."

A shadow of concern crossed his face. "I was careful how I worded it."

"Doesn't matter. I'm sure she has us halfway to the altar by now."

"I need to talk to you."

"Look, since Sam's going to be here in thirty minutes, let's concentrate on getting ready. Want to go first?"

He frowned. "You go ahead."

As she closed the bathroom door, she saw Jack hesitate, then pick up the phone. Ignoring the temptation to listen at the door, she quickly turned on the shower. She really didn't want to know what he had to say to Stephanie.

DANI TAPPED LIGHTLY on the bathroom door. "I think Mona's here. Come out decent."

Before Jack could reply, she moved to the peephole, verified that it was Mona and opened the door.

"I hope you weren't worried." Mona handed Sam over when Dani reached for him. Talcum powder filtered through the air and made Dani sneeze. Mona had used enough to choke a horse.

"Not at all." Dani smiled at Sam, giving him an extra bounce in the air. He chortled with delight.

"Jack sounded funny. Everything okay with you two?"

"Fine."

"Where is he?"

"Taking a shower."

Mona conspicuously eyed Dani's damp hair. "I can keep Sam awhile longer you know."

"No, thanks. I'll be leaving soon, anyway. I'm afraid Sam will be Jack's problem."

Mona's eyes narrowed as she shifted her gaze toward the closed bathroom door. "What's going on?"

"I called the airport. They said there's a chance some flights will be cleared for takeoff this evening. I want to be first in line."

"What about the road?"

"According to the front desk, the tide's receded and four-wheel drives have been having some luck."

"Dani, I don't think—"

"Not now, Mona." Dani dragged a weary hand across her eyes. She rarely used her mother's name. She hoped the fact that she did made it clear she wasn't open to discussion.

When she focused on her mother again, Mona's face was white and anxious, and Dani felt a new surge of affection for her. In a matter of seconds, she understood her mother better than she ever had, felt a connection that she never dreamed possible. And the sad irony twisted Dani's heart.

"I hope you aren't making a mistake, Daniella."

Me too. Dani gave her a wan smile. "I'll call you later, okay?"

Getting the message, Mona backed out into the corridor. "Call me sooner if you want," she called when Dani started to close the door.

She nodded, knowing that wouldn't happen. Her mother would never understand why she had to leave.

"Hey, buddy." Jack walked out of the bathroom and headed straight for Sam. "Where's Mona?"

Dani let go of the doorknob. "She just left."

"Damn." He took Sam from her, and noticing her arched brows, he said, "I may have to ask her to watch Sam again."

"I'm sorry I can't do it."

"I know. I'm flying you to—"

Someone pounded at the door. Loud. On the other side, a shrill, unintelligible voice punctuated the knock.

"What is this, Grand Central Station?" Frowning in the direction of the shriek, Jack handed Sam to her, then reached for the doorknob without looking through the peephole.

Cradling the baby to her, Dani stepped back when what she really wanted to do was block the door. She didn't give a flying fig who was out there. She wanted Jack to finish what he'd been about to say. As anxious as she was to leave the island, apparently she wasn't half as eager as Jack was to get rid of her.

Feeling the sting of that realization, she watched as

the door opened wide and an ashen faced Rik stood with his knuckles in midair ready to knock again.

"Where is he?" The voice shrieked from behind Rik, who stepped aside with a resigned expression.

A short blond woman barely waited for him to clear the way before she pushed past him and barged into the room. Her face was red, the whites of her eyes so bloodshot, Dani hurt just looking at her.

"Sam!" The woman charged Dani and reached for the baby. There was instant recognition as Sam laughed and kicked and hurled himself into the woman's arms. "Oh, God, Sam, are you okay?" Tears welled in her eyes, and she laughed and cried as she hugged the baby to her.

"The mother?" Jack frowned at Rik, who nodded glumly. "How did you find—"

"The big dope is my brother," the blond woman interrupted through bouts of hiccups. "Former brother, that is." She gave Rik a scathing look, then spotting Sam's basket, she grabbed it off the dresser and headed for the door. "Thanks for taking such good care of Sam."

Rik stepped aside without saying a word. Stunned, Dani stepped back, too. And from the dumbfounded look on Jack's face, she knew he was just as shocked as she was.

When the woman swept past them into the corridor without a second glance, Rik started after her. "Lynn, wait a minute. How did I know there'd be a storm?"

Jack grabbed him by the shirt to stop him. "Oh, no, you don't. What the hell were you doing?"

"Can I explain later?" Rik jammed a hand through his hair. "She's *really* ticked at me."

Jack reared his head back in irritation. "*I'm* really ticked at you, pal. What the hell is going on?"

Rik blew out a loud, exasperated breath. "Admit it. You have no business getting married."

Both men glanced at Dani. She knew she should make herself scarce as this was none of her concern, but excitement and hope kept her immobile and the best she could do was feign sudden interest in the contents of the boutique bag lying beside her on the table.

"Don't you want to talk about this later?" Rik asked, lowering his voice.

Jack folded his arms across his chest. "Now."

Rik sent her another guarded look while drawing Jack toward the bathroom. When he looked back at his friend, he laughed. One of those typical, male, no-problem laughs. "Jack, you don't want to be married. I know you. You've got too much going on."

Jack blinked and his arms slackened. With obvious reluctance, he slid Dani a brief and uncertain look. "Like what?"

"Come on, Jack, you know."

Dani didn't know if it was the wicked gleam in Rik's eyes or the mischievous, knowing tilt to his head that finally was her undoing. But she felt her confidence unravel, her fragile joy shatter.

This was Jack's best friend. The person who probably knew him best. And even if she were totally ignorant of body language or voice patterns, the message would still be loud and clear. Jack would never be happy with someone like her. As Rik said, he had too much going on. And she was just a schoolteacher—his holiday fling.

"Rik, I don't know what's got into you..." Jack

looked from his friend to Dani. Panic flooded his face. "I'm not marrying Stephanie."

Someone knocked at the still-open door. Jack swung toward the sound, biting off an earthy curse that made the young man standing there grimace.

"I have a message for Jack Keaton from Stephanie Brewster," the uniformed clerk said, holding up an envelope.

Frowning, Jack patted his pocket, located his wallet and started to dig for it.

"Never mind. It's on me." The clerk handed the message to Rik while Jack's hand was still stuffed in his pocket, then he disappeared down the corridor.

Jack studied the envelope for a moment before reaching for it. He had a reticent look on his face, almost as if he were afraid of the news. Probably because this meant Stephanie was delayed further. He'd said he wasn't marrying her. Dani didn't believe that. She'd seen the cornered look in his eyes and knew it was a spur-of-the-moment remark.

Rik was oddly silent, his rapt expression centered on his friend and the telegram. Dani felt horribly out of place. She had to get out of here. The sooner she got to the airport the better chance she had of getting to Honolulu tonight. She had to leave. Not just for the audition, but for the sake of her sanity.

Absorbed with the message, Jack started to turn his back on her and she was almost grateful. *Almost*. The unintended dismissal stung.

"Dani, would you close the door?" Jack glanced back, the strain he was under etching grooves around his mouth.

She nodded, but he didn't see. He had already turned away to slowly peel back the flap of the envelope. She took a few seconds to watch him, to sear an imprint of his profile on her mind.

He was so deep in thought that he didn't even notice when she grabbed her bag, and slipped out the door before closing it softly behind her.

JACK SKIPPED the elevator and raced down the stairs. He'd overheard someone waiting for a car say that the delays were ranging from ten to twenty minutes. If he was lucky, Dani'd had to wait long enough that he could still catch her in the lobby.

By the time he got to the second-floor landing, he thought his heart would explode in his chest. It didn't help matters that the old ticker had started pounding long before he hit the stairs. His heartbeat had gone berserk the moment Stephanie's message had sunk in.

Within seconds, he pushed open the lobby door to a sea of anxious faces and floral fabrics. People oozed from the corridors, littered the sofas, swarmed the front desk. Was every damn guest in the hotel in the damn lobby?

Heedless of the nasty stares he got, he thrust through the wave of bodies, his gaze sweeping the area with lightning speed. Dread ate at his stomach, and his pulse sprinted out of control. He had to find her.

"Jack?"

The bag he clutched nearly slipped and his heart fluttered as he turned toward the voice. A curse lodged in his throat. "Not now, Babs." He started to turn away again when over Babs's head, he saw Dani coming out of the boutique.

"Jack." Babs's voice rose sharply as he pushed past her.

But he ignored her and her husband as he nearly

tripped over a suitcase in his haste. Sidestepping a luggage cart, he vaulted over a cluster of shopping bags, then hopped on his left foot when he came down too hard on his right.

"Dani!" His voice rose above the excited buzz of anxious tourists but still she hurried toward the front doors without turning around.

Ignoring the pain in his ankle, he quickly limped toward the lobby entrance in order to cut her off. He was about to call out to her again when, as if sensing his presence, she stopped and turned around.

He wasn't sure if she saw him at first. Her gaze swept the crowd, and the sadness he saw in her eyes made him ache. Her ponytail was slightly askew, and she was still wearing his too-large shirt. She never looked better.

When her attention finally settled on him, the sadness slipped away and the smile that lighted up her face gave him courage. And then it was gone.

Taking a deep breath, he limped toward her. Her gaze slid to his feet. "What happened?" she asked.

"You."

Her eyes widened to meet his. "I've got to go."

"I told you I'd fly you to Honolulu."

"That's not necessary. I'll make sure you get your clothes back by tomorrow morning. Goodbye, Jack." She turned away.

He laid a hand on her arm. "You forgot something."

Although she hesitated, tension hummed through the warm skin beneath his fingers. He clenched his teeth, trapping the air in his throat, not sure she'd face him again.

"What?" Slowly she turned around. Her eyes had

darkened to that deep mossy green, where fear tangled with regret, anticipation with dread.

"Here." He extended the bag he'd been clutching.

"What is it?" she asked, eyeing it with a skeptical lift of her chin.

"Open it."

She blinked, drawing her lower lip between her teeth, then reached for the bag and quickly withdrew the white dress. Disappointment, then anger, stormed her face.

"You know how I feel about this dress—"

Looking directly into her thunderous gaze, he held up a hand and said, "I'm willing to wait."

She didn't say anything. She merely stared back— stunned, confused, reluctant—the dress hanging from her lifeless hand.

"You'll get tired of traveling sooner or later. Adventure is way overrated, believe me." He smiled and when he took her other hand, he was relieved she didn't pull away. "It's going to take me a while to wrap up the business and for me to find—"

"What about Stephanie?"

He thought about the "Dear John" telegram tucked in his pocket. Stephanie had found her soul mate while waiting out the hurricane at the Honolulu airport. He hoped she was even half as happy as Dani had made him. "I already told you I wasn't marrying her."

"But what—?"

"Do you really want to talk about this in the middle of the lobby? Let me fly you to Honolulu."

"That's not necessary."

His heart thudded. So much for making progress. "So you said. I just thought that would buy us a little more time to talk."

"I'm not going to Honolulu." A slight frown drew her brows together, and Jack thought he saw hope there. "Tell me about this dress."

"What do you mean you're not going to Honolulu? When did you decide that?"

"Back in your room. Now, about the dress..."

Jack felt like he'd been kicked in the gut by a runaway packmule. "Why?"

"I had enough adventure in the last two days. Boring isn't so bad."

His heart beat double time. "So you wouldn't mind being married to a boring football coach?"

"Depends who he is."

Smiling, Jack pulled her toward him. "Will the luckiest guy in the world do?"

"Boring is okay but I really hate clichés."

"Did I tell you cheeky women annoy the hell out of me?"

Her grin faltered. "We don't know each other very well, do we?"

"I know all I need to know. You have a great sense of humor. You like kids. You're generous and smart. And you don't squeeze the toothpaste from the middle of the tube." He kissed her firmly on the mouth until his body tightened with need. "And the chemistry isn't bad either."

"I'll come to the Amazon with you," she said, her voice breathless.

"I love you, Dani Carpenter."

She tilted her head back, her expression soft with emotion. "I love you, Jack."

He hugged her closer until her heart pounded against his. "It'll take at least six months to wrap everything up. Maybe longer."

"I took a year's sabbatical."

"We'll get married before we leave. Today maybe."

She pulled back, her eyes wide. "Before we leave?"

He took the dress from her hand and shook it out. "You wanna know something else about me, Dr. Carpenter? I know how to iron." He grabbed her hand and started threading a path through the crowd toward the elevators.

"Maybe I should wear the Big Bird costume."

He laughed. "And I'll ask Sam to be my best man."

Dani stopped, and she tugged for him to stop, too. "I know who I want for my maid of honor."

He followed her gaze. A handkerchief covering her nose, Mona stood several yards away watching them. One false eyelash was seriously out of whack but she continued to sniffle heedlessly.

"She did a great job of raising you," Jack said.

"I know," Dani whispered, and gave her mom a thumbs-up sign.

Epilogue

"I never want to see another mosquito for as long as I live." Dani settled into her first class plane seat, closed her eyes and sighed with the sheer pleasure of having something soft under her bottom.

Jack chuckled. "Then maybe we ought to think about moving to Alaska. Do they have mosquitoes there?"

"Hawaiian mosquitoes will be fine with me. At least they're civilized."

"Of course."

Dani opened her eyes to stare into her husband's laughing face, and she grinned. "I felt bad at first, thinking I was dragging you away from all that. But now I know the truth. I'm actually saving you."

Nodding solemnly, he picked her hand up off the armrest and kissed her palm. "No doubt one of those bloodthirsty suckers would have snatched me up and carted me off."

She laughed and pulled her hand away to brush back the long shaggy lock of hair that fell across his forehead. He hadn't been to a barber in months. She'd whacked at his mane herself a few haphazard times—enough to know she could never make a living as a stylist. But now they were returning to civilization. Life would change drastically for him in the coming months. Just as life had changed for her in the jungle.

"Jack, are you sure—"

He put a silencing finger to her lips. "You know what the best thing about living in the Amazon together for nine months was? Getting to know each other."

She nodded, watching the familiar way one side of his mouth lifted. It was the truth. There had been plenty of rough times along with the good ones. Their relationship had been tested often. And they had managed to come out ahead, their senses of humor intact.

"So, having said that, you tell me what you think," he added patiently. "Am I ready to leave the jungle? Am I ready to coach college football?"

Reassured, she smiled. "But the real question is, are you ready to be a father?"

He leaned back in his seat and stared dumbly at her. "You mean...we're going to have a Sam?"

"Is that what you want to name her?"

"What if she's a him?"

Dani laughed. "Then we can still name him Sam." Then she sobered. "Do you think it's too soon to start a family?"

"For us?" Jack slipped an arm around her shoulders and hugged her. "Honey, I think we're right on schedule."

EVER HAD ONE OF THOSE DAYS?

TO DO:

☑ at the supermarket buying two dozen muffins that your son just remembered to tell you he needed for the school treat, you realize you left your wallet at home

☑ at work just as you're going into the big meeting, you discover your son took your presentation to school, and you have his hand-drawn superhero comic book

☑ your mother-in-law calls to say she's coming for a month-long visit

☑ finally at the end of a long and exasperating day, you escape from it all with an entertaining, humorous and always romantic Love & Laughter book!

ENJOY
LOVE & LAUGHTER™
EVERY DAY!

For a preview, turn the page....

*Here's a sneak peek at
Carrie Alexander's THE AMOROUS HEIRESS
Available September 1997...*

"YOU'RE A VERY popular lady," Jed Kelley observed as Augustina closed the door on her suitors.

She waved a hand. "Just two of a dozen." Technically true since her grandmother had put her on the open market. "You're not afraid of a little competition, are you?"

"Competition?" He looked puzzled. "I thought the position was mine."

Augustina shook her head, smiling coyly. "You didn't think Grandmother was the final arbiter of the decision, did you? I say a trial period is in order." No matter that Jed Kelley had miraculously passed Grandmother's muster, Augustina felt the need for a little propriety. But, on the other hand, she could be married before the summer was out and be free as a bird, with the added bonus of a husband it wouldn't be all that difficult to learn to love.

She got up the courage to reach for his hand, and then just like that, she—Miss Gussy Gutless Fairchild—was holding Jed Kelley's hand. He looked down at their linked hands. "Of course, you don't really know what sort of work I can do, do you?"

A funny way to put it, she thought absently, cradling

his callused hand between both of her own. "We can get to know each other, and then, if that works out..." she murmured. *Wow.* If she'd known what this arranged marriage thing was all about, she'd have been a supporter of Grandmother's campaign from the start!

"Are you a palm reader?" Jed asked gruffly. His voice was as raspy as sandpaper and it was rubbing her all the right ways, but the question flustered her. She dropped his hand.

"I'm sorry."

"No problem," he said, "as long as I'm hired."

"Hired!" she scoffed. "What a way of putting it!"

Jed folded his arms across his chest. "So we're back to the trial period."

"Yes." Augustina frowned and her gaze dropped to his work boots. Okay, so he wasn't as well off as the majority of her suitors, but really, did he think she was going to *pay* him to marry her?

"Fine, then." He flipped her a wave and, speechless, she watched him leave. She was trembling all over like a malaria victim in a snowstorm, shot with hot charges and cold shivers until her brain was numb. This couldn't be true. Fantasy men didn't happen to nice girls like her.

"Augustina?"

Her grandmother's voice intruded on Gussy's privacy. "Ahh. There you are. I see you met the new gardener?"

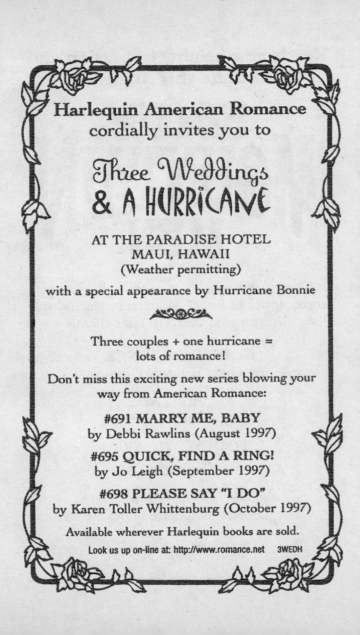

Harlequin American Romance
cordially invites you to

Three Weddings & A HURRICANE

AT THE PARADISE HOTEL
MAUI, HAWAII
(Weather permitting)

with a special appearance by Hurricane Bonnie

Three couples + one hurricane =
lots of romance!

Don't miss this exciting new series blowing your
way from American Romance:

#691 MARRY ME, BABY
by Debbi Rawlins (August 1997)

#695 QUICK, FIND A RING!
by Jo Leigh (September 1997)

#698 PLEASE SAY "I DO"
by Karen Toller Whittenburg (October 1997)

Available wherever Harlequin books are sold.

Reach new heights of passion and
adventure this August in

ROCKY MOUNTAIN MEN

Don't miss this exciting new collection featuring
three stories of Rocky Mountain men and the
women who dared to tame them.

CODE OF SILENCE
by Linda Randall Wisdom

SILVER LADY
by Lynn Erickson

TOUCH THE SKY
by Debbi Bedford

Available this August wherever
Harlequin and Silhouette books are sold.

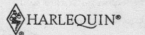 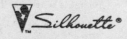

HARLEQUIN WOMEN KNOW ROMANCE WHEN THEY SEE IT.

And they'll see it on **ROMANCE CLASSICS**, the new 24-hour TV channel devoted to romantic movies and original programs like the special **Harlequin** Showcase of Authors & Stories.

The **Harlequin** Showcase of Authors & Stories introduces you to many of your favorite romance authors in a program developed exclusively for Harlequin readers.

Watch for the **Harlequin** Showcase of **Authors & Stories** series beginning in the summer of 1997.

If you're not receiving ROMANCE CLASSICS,
call your local cable operator or satellite provider
and ask for it today!

Escape to the network of your dreams.

Let's Celebrate!

LOVE & LAUGHTER™

invites you to
the party of the season!

Grab your popcorn and be prepared to laugh
as we celebrate with **LOVE & LAUGHTER**.

Harlequin's newest series is going Hollywood!

Let us make you laugh with three months of terrific
books, authors and romance, plus a chance to win a
FREE 15-copy video collection of the best romantic
comedies ever made.

For more details look in the back pages of any
Love & Laughter title, from July to September,
at your favorite retail outlet.

Don't forget the popcorn!

Available wherever
Harlequin books are sold.

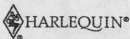 HARLEQUIN®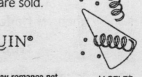

Look us up on-line at: http://www.romance.net

LLCELEB